My

First

Pair

of

Shorts

My First Short

The Elevator

The Elevator

"Wake up my son, time to get ready for school."

"Mom, is that you?"

"Yes, dear and it is six and time to get up, first day of school and you have to get ready."

"Must I get up?"

"Yes Stuart, I'm going downstairs and will make breakfast."

Those words from my mom still are fresh in my mind, pretty crazy because that was the start of my senior year in High School. So I guess you would like to know why my mom was talking to me like I was a little kid even though I was seventeen years old. Well, not really sure why but I guess it had to do with her not wanting me to grow up but that is only a guess, never did I ask her. I struggled to wake up but when I finally was wide-awake, I had a great feeling inside and was so delighted to start the school year. I was so ready to put the past three months behind me; I had the worst summer, which started on my way home from my last day of school back in early June.

My best friend Jackson Johnson and I were acting like most boys who had just finished our next to last year of High School would act, you know just being guys acting like we were already seniors and being show offs. He and I left school and already had chips on our shoulders and we were making it known to our younger schoolmates that they were going to have to watch their step around us in the next school year. JJ, that was Jackson's nickname and he and I were really good students throughout all the years we were in school. JJ's family moved next door to me when I was in the fourth grade and this was by far the most significant factor to changing my personality and in the most positive way possible.

Before JJ, I was quiet, reserved and let me say, a not so cool kid even though it was only in grade school. JJ was well, I'm trying to think of the best way to put it so I have the following analogy to describe how he brought out the best in me that was not present until we met. So, here it goes... JJ was like a surgeon who used a scalpel to cut deep into my gut and then he reached in and found the devil that was sitting dormant and pulled him out. Not sure if this makes sense but as I said, I was a quiet and reserved kid but after hanging around JJ for all these years, I distinctly remember that it was right after I turned sixteen; I flipped and if I was previously like an angel, now I was anything but. Like I said in my analogy, he pulled the devil out from within and now I was nothing like I was before. Quiet now, no way! Reserved, no way! I was now like the center of attention and along with JJ; we made sure that everyone knew it. I was like a bull in a china shop and it seemed that I was now one that would not let anyone push me around; I felt like I was it, if you know what I mean.

As I was saying, JJ and I left school and we were both so ready for the summer break. We were walking home but JJ had something planned for us and I was shocked when he told me what he had up his sleeves.

"Come on Stuart, I have something for us to do on our way home."

"Really, come on JJ, I told my mom I would be home right after school."

"Well, that will not be the case, we are seniors in High School and we need to get ready to show all the others in school that we are the top dogs in school."

"So, you have this something that we are going to do to make us these dogs?"

"That's top dogs Stu, not just dogs."

"Alright JJ, so what are we going to do to be these top dogs?"

"Just follow my lead, we are making a bit of a detour to the mall."

"Alright, but for what?"

"Man, you ask a lot of questions; just trust me and be cool."

This being cool was still a bit new to me, "Alright JJ, I can be cool, let's go."

I followed JJ and we walked roughly a mile out of our way to the mall; I still had no idea what he was up to but I was definitely there for the ride. I quickly made up my mind that I would be cool and not act like the goofy kid I used to be.

"So where are we going JJ?"

"You'll see."

We entered the mall and then it was a short walk to the one and only department store and we just roamed around and I still had no idea what or why we were here. This store had three floors and three elevators, two in the front and one in the back. The doors to the elevators in the front were both brightly decorated and the cool thing about the back elevator was that it was connected to an office building. I had never used the elevators; I always took the escalators located in the center of the store as they took me to where I needed to go.

"So tell me JJ, why are we here?"

"Just chill Stuart, you'll know why in a bit."

"Alright, I'll chill."

We continued to walk around the store; a tall man wearing a burgundy suit spoke out to us, "Welcome and if you need any assistance, please check back with me or any of our other Customer Service Reps."

This man had a deep voice and I turned around and replied, "Thank you and if I need anything I will look for you."

"Enjoy your day and please check out the sales items on the second floor."

"Thank you sir and you are?"

"Flanigan, Frank Flanigan."

"Glad to meet you and my friend and I will check out the sales." I looked over to JJ and he gave me a little push and I knew that it was time to move on.

We continued our walk; I was still wondering why he brought me here. "Come on JJ, what's going on here?"

JJ didn't answer but then as we walked up to the jewelry department, he abruptly stopped. He looked to his left, then to his right and then grabbed a couple of watches that were on display and put one in his pocket and to my surprise, put the other one in the jacket I was wearing. I started to say something but he tugged on my jacket and we quickly walked off.

I didn't know what to do and I was scared, I had never stolen anything before. Well that is not actually true, there was candy that I stole but I was maybe nine when it happened. What we were doing now was nothing like stealing candy. I figured that the watches were like fifty bucks each; we were in the act of serious stealing!

"Come on Stu, we have one more stop and then we are going upstairs."

I was speechless and then as we were almost out of the jewelry department, crazy JJ swiped a couple of charm bracelets that were on these spinning racks. They didn't look to be expensive, not like the watches but once again he put one into my jacket. Still shocked by his actions all I could do was to follow him; I wanted to say something but that something was nowhere near the tip of my tongue. He and I walked rather fast and to the elevator in the back of the store. I was actually a bit out of breath, my asthma had kicked in and I was wheezing a bit as JJ pushed the elevator's button to go up. I was anxious and JJ, well he was as cool as a cucumber as we waited for the elevator to arrive.

I leaned over to JJ, "What got into you, why are you doing this?"

"Come on Stu, don't let that old dreary kid come back, we are cool guys, and this will prove to others just how cool we are."

"But stealing isn't a way to make us cool, we need to show how cool we are by being good students, respect worthy, doing things for others and..."

JJ interrupted me as the elevator doors opened, "Quick Stu, let's get in, we need to pick up something on the second floor."

I made my way into the elevator wondering what else JJ had up his sleeves but before I could say anything to him, the elevator doors quickly shut and JJ was still on the other side. I pushed the button to open the door but it didn't do anything. I pushed it again and again but still nothing other than the elevator began to move and there was an odd sound and smell like a motor was ready to burn out. I heard the gears of the elevator churning away and slowly it moved and then it stopped and the floor indicator above the elevator showed it was on the second floor.

The doors opened and a man was standing right outside of the elevator and with a resounding deep melodic voice said, "Welcome to North Shore Dining Room, your table sir is waiting."

The Elevator

I walked out and this was odd, nothing was right, this was not the second floor of the department store, it was a restaurant and I could see the ocean at the far end of this dining room. One word to describe this and that was weird, very weird.

This man walked me around several sections of this very fine-looking dining room and I was quite confused but at the same time impressed by my surroundings. Most impressive were the women who were not like me, what I mean is that they were real grownups and not one but all were drop down gorgeous. They were all different shapes, tall and short and all different ethnicities. I felt like I was in the middle of a fashion show, elegant clothing on display on all of these beautiful women. I knew I was gawking at the amazing sites I had ever seen and the last thing on my mind was how this was all happening; I totally forgot that I was in the department store. I continued to gaze around the room and then this dude stopped at this one table.

"Here you are sir, your date Lynn will be right over to join you, she had to leave but asked that I seat you and to let you know to wait. May I take your jacket?"

I was dumbfounded by all that was going on and then it came to me that I surely didn't want this total stranger to get his hands on my jacket, after all I did have the stolen items in one of the pockets. I didn't want to bring about any suspicion, I politely replied,

"I think I'll hold onto my jacket, it might be a bit chilly later on and thank you for bringing me to the table."

This guy nodded and walked away and I gawked at all the people in the room; no not really, I only paid attention to the gals, not the guys. The room itself had dark maple flooring and the walls were a light tan. Beach-like items were hanging from the tall ceilings, you know like surfboards, beach balls, even beach chairs and lounges. This was so cool and the best part, other than the women, was that only a matter of maybe twenty feet away was a floor to ceiling window and a deck on the other side of it and then the most beautiful deep blue ocean I had ever seen. My thoughts of where I was or how I got here were long gone and then things got even better when I was tapped on my right shoulder.

"Hello Stuart, I'm Lynn and I have been waiting for you."

I stood up and went to shake her hand.

Her voice was very soft and sweet, "What is that about?" She leaned over to me and kissed me on my cheek. "So be a gentleman and take me to my seat."

I had never been in a position like this before but I remembered back to watching movies and seeing the scenes when a man would pull out the chair and let the woman sit down and gently push the chair in toward the table. I stood up and did just that and was in total awe of this woman and as I walked back to my chair. I couldn't take my eyes off of her and as I was sitting down, I sat on the edge and fell off the chair.

Lynn laughed and others around the room were chuckling at my true act of being dumb.

With concern in her voice, Lynn asked me, "Are you alright my dear Stuart?"

I stood up and felt my face was as red as a ripe tomato, "Yes, I'm fine." I then took my seat and knew that I was staring; she was breathtaking. I looked so underdressed with my jeans and T-Shirt; Lynn was wearing a mid length dark navy-blue skirt with a tan short sleeved blouse. Her long curly blonde hair was down to her shoulders and her face, well it was as perfect as perfect could be, so angelical. I was mesmerized and didn't say anything but caught myself as I let out a loud sigh which I'm sure she heard as well as others sitting nearby. I then had to quickly get my act together and said, "I am so pleased to meet you Lynn and you are a vision of pure beauty."

She smiled and laughingly said, "Come on Stuart, to be with me means that you have to loosen up, let your inhibitions go by the wayside."

Lynn then reached into her purse and pulled out her makeup bag and from within, took out a small mirror. She first looked at herself and smiled and moved the few long blonde hairs that were just slightly out of place and hanging over her forehead and toward her beautiful deep blue eyes. I felt my jaw was dropping and then she looked at me and handed me the mirror.

"My dear Stu, please take a look at yourself."

I took the mirror and when I looked at myself, I saw this seventeen year-old kid with his hair all messed up from the fall. With my hand, I quickly pushed the misplaced hairs back into place and returned the mirror to Lynn. I was a bit of a basket case and putting the best sentence together was not something that I seemed capable of. I stuttered out, "Thank thank you and menus, we should ask the the guy for the menus."

Lynn reached over to me and took my hand, "Relax love, you are going to be just fine this evening. I will get the attention of the hostess and get the menus and know that I will be with you throughout the evening."

Her voice was so soothing and I was melting in my chair listening to her words and wondering what she was actually saying to me. I wasn't used to hearing anything like this before from any of the girls my age in school and I was guessing that Lynn was in her twenties.

I gripped her hand a bit tighter and she looked at me, "Stuart, please relax, I am not going anywhere and you are in good hands with me. And by the way, I am twenty-three."

How did she know that I was wondering how old she was? I guess it didn't matter how but wow, I was with a woman not like me in my teens but a real woman and a grown woman in her twenties. How did I get so lucky? I loosened my grip and took a deep breath, then another and upon exhaling Lynn took my hand and reached to her face and kissed it. I was in a state of shock.

"Much better Stuart, please just be you and let everything that happens tonight unfold in a most wonderful, natural and beautiful way, alright my dear?"

What could I possibly say after her kiss to my hand and her words were like words spoken by well, my analogy would be her words were like a bird chirping happily in springtime. I didn't know what to say but then the words just fell from my lips, "How about we skip the meal and head out to the beach?" I was looking toward Lynn and was amazed with the words that came out of my mouth.

Lynn smiled, "Yes, let's go and walk the beach barefoot and have the sand fall between our toes."

My mind was rushing, "Come on, let's get out of here".

With that, we left the dining room holding hands and walked to the back and I opened the wooden gate to the deck. There were other couples eating there and others just walking but for me, there was only one couple that really mattered and that was Lynn and I. I was so happy, after all, look who I was with, the most amazingly beautiful woman in the whole restaurant and I could feel the looks coming my way. I felt like I was on top of the mountain, the king of the forest, the toy that was within the box of Cracker Jacks, and, well you get the analogy as to how I felt. Simply put, I enjoyed being with Lynn and for the first time, I felt respect from the guys that I could tell were looking at me with envy after all, I was with this vision of pure beauty. Sure these guys were all strangers but it didn't matter to me, I was truly happy and it was all due to Lynn.

We walked to the far end of the deck to the private entrance to the beach. This restaurant was quite thoughtful regarding taking care of their customers; a wooden shoe rack was right next to the gate to the beach. The shoe rack had individual cubby holes for shoes and in each was the security card to get back in from the beach. I removed my tennis shoes and socks and Lynn; well let me tell you, seeing her taking off her high heel shoes was quite a sight to see. She was struggling, there was no chair or stool to sit on so I quickly manned up and stood next to her and with my arm around her shapely waist, I provided the balance for her to take her heels off; once off, she was now a couple of inches shorter than me. I took her heels and my tennis shoes with the socks inside and placed them in one of the cubbyholes and took the security card. Holding hands again, we walked a few feet to the gate and after unlocking it, we walked down the three steps to the beach and it felt so wonderful; I placed the security card into my right pocket of my pants. We were both like kids; we dug our feet into the sand and enjoyed the feeling as the sand was now covering our feet. We then began to walk the depth of the beach to the water, which I guessed was about a hundred feet.

The sun was slowly setting and there was a slight breeze as we made our way to the edge of the water, neither of us put our feet into the water. I was feeling so wonderful, after all, here I was on this most spectacular beach with the sun setting and with a stunning woman and holding hands like there was no tomorrow; what more could a guy ask for?

A couple minutes passed; we turned back toward the deck when all of a sudden the wind came up. It was just a slight breeze but enough that I could tell that Lynn was chilled by it. I let go of her hand and took my jacket off and reached into the pocket where JJ had placed the watch and bracelet; I didn't feel them. I dug around a bit more only to realize I was on the wrong side of the jacket; I reached into the other pocket and was relieved as they were there. I didn't think twice about the thievery that previously took place. I was the consummate gentleman, I placed my jacket over Lynn's shoulders and without hesitation I wrapped my arm around her waist. Lynn in turn put her head on my shoulder and we continued to walk the beach.

All of a sudden, a woman's voice screamed out, "Help me, help me!"

My attention instantly moved from Lynn as I turned around to look in the direction the voice came from.

The woman screamed out again, "Someone help me, please help me!"

I continued looking but didn't see anyone however; I knew what I had to do. I abruptly let go of Lynn and yelled toward this unknown woman, "I am on my way!"

Lynn grabbed my arm and with a raised voice yelled out, "You're not going anywhere Stuart. You are with me and no other woman should be on your mind, much less you would even think about wanting to leave my side."

I looked at her and was totally amazed by what she said, "What is wrong with you? She is screaming out for help and you don't want me to do anything about it?"

With steam in her voice Lynn replied, "Yes, that's right. You and I are together and let's go back to the deck."

"The woman yelled out again, "Hurry, please hurry!"

I pulled away from Lynn, "Sorry, I need to go."

As I was running off, Lynn yelled out, "You leave me and don't even bother thinking of coming back to me!"

I didn't reply, I ran back down the beach and it was just a bit past the furthest point that Lynn and I had just walked from. The woman yelled out again, "Anyone, please help me!"

I yelled out, "Keep talking, I will find you but you need to guide me to where you are."

"By the rocks, I'm sitting on the rocks."

I saw them and continued to run toward them but as soon as I reached the rocky area, I had to walk very carefully and being barefoot didn't help matters. "I'm here, where are you," I yelled out.

"I see you; I'm sitting on a large rock that is in the water."

I saw what she was referring to and cautiously worked my way down to the water and saw her. Only a couple more feet through the chilly water and jagged rocks and at last I reached her. I sat down next to her; the water was about up to my calves.
Her voice was shaky and I could feel her pain, "Thank you, thank you so much."

She began to cry hysterically, I put my arms around her to comfort her, "What happened?"

With pain in her words, "I was out for a swim and missed judged the depth of the water and the terrain. As I was getting out of the water, out of nowhere, I felt something hit me from behind and whatever it was, I was knocked to the ground."

I looked around and saw a surfboard floating on top of the shallow water not too far away from where we were sitting. I looked back at this woman and there was a rather large mark on her back and knew that the surfboard was the culprit. I also saw blood coming from a cut to her right foot and by her toes and with a concerned voice, "Can you stand up?"

"I tried but fell back down and when I did, I felt something in my right ankle."

"This might hurt but try to lift your foot so I can see what's going on."

She leaned back, bracing herself against another rock and raised her leg and extended her foot. I gently took it into my hands and even though I was not qualified at all to make a diagnosis, it was as clear as clear could be; her ankle was swollen and I just knew that it was broken. The blood was still coming and I was able to see that there was about an inch cut just below her toes; I knew I had to do something and time was of the essence.

"What do you see?"

I was calm and didn't want to panic her. With a soothing voice I replied, "Well, let me say that you probably won't be dancing anytime soon, let's get you out of here."

"Alright but…"

"Don't even say anything, just hang on."

I stood up and in one quick move; I picked her up and carefully moved through the rugged rocks and then to the sandy beach. "By the way, what's your name?"

"It's Bonnie, and I was in one of your classes a couple of years ago."

I felt so stupid and didn't know what on earth I could say to her so I lied through my teeth, "I remember you, didn't you used to have short hair and you sat in the front row of the science class?"

"Sorry Stuart, I know you don't remember me and that's fine. By the way, it wasn't science, it was a math class and my hair was long, not short.

With that I figured it was best just for me to shut up and concentrate on getting Bonnie back to the deck and then into the restaurant. Besides, I was having a hard time talking and walking at the same time. As far as carrying Bonnie, there was a part of me that was enjoying it, after all she was my age, very cute and she did seem to be rather cool. Well, as cool as one could be with blood dripping from her foot and a possible broken ankle and oh yes, one heck of a bruise on her back.

We were almost at the entrance to the deck, "Bonnie, can you reach into my right pocket of my pants?"

She laughed through her pain, "Isn't that something we would do on a date?"

I chuckled, "I need the gate card, and who knows what will happen next."

She reached into my pocket and pulled out the card. I turned around in the best way for her to tap it on the gate sensor, it opened and I walked up the three steps. It was so cool, I was holding onto Bonnie and she had her arms draped around me. I carried her to a lounge chair and gently laid her down. I then looked at her and my emotions were running so fast; it was like I was on a roller coaster and had just gone up to the highest high point of the ride, only to be dropped down and to the lowest low point. My shirt and jeans were drenched and I was shivering but that hardly mattered at all; I was only concerned that Bonnie would get the help that she needed.

"So, you left me for this girl Stuart?"

Just my luck, it was Lynn, "Well, she needed help and what was I to do?"

Lynn took off my jacket and threw it at me. I caught it and with a smile I sarcastically said, "Thank you, I need to put it over Bonnie."

She yelled back at me, "Well fine, and goodbye!"

I didn't even bother replying to her as I draped my jacket over Bonnie. At the same time, there were others that had come to the deck to check out the commotion and one was the restaurant manager who immediately saw what was going on and called 911 for an ambulance. He told us that help would be here in just a few minutes. A waiter was standing next to us and picked up a cloth napkin from a dining table and poured water onto it, he then used it to clean up the blood on Bonnie's foot and toes. A waitress helped as well by bringing water for both of us. Lynn, well she was long gone and I held onto Bonnie and was not going to let her go.

I heard the siren and within minutes, help had arrived. The paramedics worked their way through the tables on the deck and to the lounge chair. I was still holding onto Bonnie's hand; I leaned down and kissed her on her forward and said, "The paramedics are here and they are going to take care of you, you will be in good hands."

I had to let go of her hand as she was picked up and placed on the stretcher and then with a smile and her soft voice resonating into my soul she said, "I feel that I have already been in real good caring hands."

I smiled at her and reached out for her hand; a wonderful feeling came over me but I had to let go as the paramedics were doing their job, you know like checking out her condition. They handed me my jacket and then placed a blanket on top of Bonnie and in just a matter of minutes, we were on our way through the deck and into the dining room and to the elevator. I walked in front and was the first to reach the elevator, I pushed the button for down and we all waited. I leaned over and this time I kissed her on her cheek, "You are such a beautiful girl and I shall never forget this evening."

The doors opened and I quickly went inside and pushed the button to keep them from closing. Bonnie turned her head as the paramedics were just about to wheel her in as she said, "From the first time I met you in school, you were always so…"

Just then, the elevator doors slammed shut and I was alone and frantically pushed the open door button but nothing, nothing at all happened. I was in a state of panic, Bonnie with the paramedics were still on the other side. Again, I pushed the button to open the doors; the elevator then started to move. This was so weird; I didn't even push a button that would cause it to move but it was going up. The smell of the burning motor was back along with the grinding noise and then the elevator abruptly came to a stop and it jolted me forward. The light inside went out and the open door button was not working. It was so hot inside and I began to sweat and my heart was pounding. Everything that just happened between me, Lynn and Bonnie quickly vanished from my mind.

Suddenly, just as the doors had slammed shut, they opened and I was now on the third floor and in front of me was a beautiful plush garden filled with a variety of trees, plants and flowers. I was mesmerized by this beauty and took a couple of steps out as the elevator doors closed; I was now standing on bright green soft grass, the sky was a deep blue and the air was fresh. I was trying to wrap my head around yet another weird thing happening in my life; what on earth was going on with me?

I looked around and not too far away was a white gazebo with one red chair inside. I took a few more steps into the garden and then all of a sudden, a large bird flew right over me and then another one and another flew right toward my face. Then there were more birds and they were relentless; I took my jacket off and waved it in the air to fend them off but it didn't help. I was now being attacked and dropped my jacket; I began to wave my arms and hands in front of my face to protect my eyes. I was doing my best to chase off these aggressive birds but nothing helped. What on earth was going on here? What was the deal with the birds?

My reflex at that moment was to quickly leave where I was and started to run as fast as I could to the gazebo, the birds seemed to be following me; I tripped and took quite a fall and hit my head on the wood banister that was around the entire perimeter of the gazebo. I dropped to the ground; it took me a couple of minutes to pull myself up and clear the cobwebs from my head.

I stood up and looked around, there were so many birds and they were all perched peacefully on the banister around the gazebo and they were chirping. I stumbled to the red chair inside the gazebo and took several deep breaths to help me calm down.

All of a sudden a deep voice spoke out, "Stuart, welcome to the park."

"Who said that?"

"Look to your right, it was me."

I looked but didn't see anyone.

"Come on Stuart; don't be dumb, you looked to your left. I said to your right."

I actually did feel dumb and turned this time to my right but still no one was there. "Okay, now who is here, who spoke out to me?"

"You see the bag on the floor that is moving? It is next to the opening."

I looked and saw three other openings, "Which one?"

"Listen to what I said, the one with the bag that is moving!"

The voice was loud and I sensed anger. "Now wait a minute, there are three openings and each has a bag next to the door, so how about being a bit friendlier and precise with your directions and why am I talking to the thin air?"

Yelling back at me, "Look at the bags, one by one and just one of them will be moving and that is the one you want to go to. Now look!"

I looked and was a bit spooked out by this whole thing; I focused in on one bag then another and then as I looked at the last one, it was moving. "Alright, I see the bag moving now what?"

"Well, go to the bag and open it up?'

"You got to be kidding me. You want me to open the bag and then I will see what?"

"Yes, do it, I know you want to."

I got up from the chair and walked to the moving bag, I bent over and picked it up and as I opened it, a bright big green frog jumped out!

With a joyous voice the frog spoke out, "Thank you Stuart, I have been in that bag for such a long time; I'm free!"

I sat down on the floor and looked at this frog, "You are talking to me, aren't you?"

"Yes and you catch on fast."

"But frogs don't talk."

"Guess you are wrong, aren't you?"

"Well, guess so. How about you tell me where I am?"

"How about you first tell me about the watch and charm bracelet you have in your jacket?"

"I don't know what you are talking about and I'm not wearing a jacket."

The frog replied, "Alright Stuart, so this is the game you want to play with me; fine, just fine."

"No game, I don't know what you are talking about."

"We all know what you and JJ did but we won't tell the authorities as long as you follow our instructions."

I looked around and questioned the frog, "What do you mean by our instructions?"

Just my luck, a smarty pants frog that was talking back to me. "Our, means that there is more than one. Usually the word our is used in a sentence to indicate that it is belonging to or relating to us. Do I have to define instructions to you?"

I couldn't believe that a talking frog was schooling me. "I get what you are saying frog, do you have a name?"

"Yes, my name is Frank."

"Really, you are Frank?"

"Yes, frank as being direct and that is also my name. In the bag to your left is Carrie Caterpillar and the bag to her right is Sam."

"Please, please don't tell me that Sam is a snake, I hate snakes!"

"No Stuart, Sam is a snail."

"Tell me Frank, do they talk like you?'

"No, not at all. Carrie is rather shy and Sam talks but by the time he says something you feel like you want to take a nap; he is really slow in his delivery."

"So they do talk?"

"But not like me, I'm quick and use my words wisely while the others are…"

I interrupted Frank, "Alright, I get what you are saying. Yes they talk but not the same way as you do."

"Isn't that what I said? Tell me Stuart, do you have a hearing problem?"

This green frog had me and I knew that it would be best to move on and get away from talking about how a frog, caterpillar and snail were able to talk. For that matter, why did I even care how they talked?

"Let's move over to chair Stuart; we want to talk to you."

I was leery but walked over to the chair and as I sat down, I watched as Sam the snail, Carrie the caterpillar and Frank the frog slowly joined me. I felt it best to leave the chair and sit on the floor; it would be best to be on their level. "So guys, what's the scoop on you talking?"

A small voice spoke out, "Not just guys Stuart, I am a girl."

I looked and sure enough, shy Carrie was critical of my choice of words. "Forgive me Carrie; let me rephrase what I was saying. So guys and gal, what's the scoop on you talking?"

There was silence and I wasn't sure what to say or do so I waited and waited and then Sam slowly said, "We need your help with the animals in the zoo; we have a riot going on."

With skepticism I replied, "Really, a riot going on in the zoo?"

The Elevator

Frank's voice was so sincere, "Yes, there are problems that have been going on for months with the zookeeper's and management and it has affected the animals. It seems that we all do not have a voice."

I was trying my best not to chuckle, "Come on Frank, the animals do not feel they have a voice, you got to be messing with me".

Frank sighed, "Seriously Stuart, we feel hurt, abused, not cared for, and even being taking advantage of."

This was so bizarre and then to make matters even crazier than they were, Sam continued, "Best if you follow us to the zoo, you will see for yourself."

"Thank you Sam but I have no intention to go to the zoo; this is all too crazy and the three of you are bringing me deeper and deeper into your little game that you are playing with my head."

In unison they said, "No game, this is all real."

Frank continued, "Are you going to help us and our friends or are you going to be a non doer and just sit back and let others suffer?"

Wow, did he hit me below the belt or what? These three sure threw a lot of guilt my way and it worked; I knew what I had to do.

"Alright you three, I have an analogy for you."

Carrie said, "You have an apology for us?"

"What are you apologizing for?" questioned Sam.

Frank laughed out, "Come on guys, Stuart said analogy, not apology!"

Carrie seemed to understand, "Thank you Frank for clearing that up."

"You're welcome Carrie; go ahead Stuart, what is your analogy?"

"So this is simple to follow, I saw a sign that said free cookies. The cookies looked scrumptious and I really wanted to take a couple of them but next to them was a picture of a family that had recently lost everything they had in a storm. How could I enjoy something when they had nothing, I knew I had to share."

Carrie nodded, "I get it Stuart, you knew it was better to give than to receive, right Stuart?"

Before I could respond Sam added, "The sign talked?"

Frank shook his head and then Sam continued, "Were they chocolate chip?"

I wasn't sure what Sam was asking, "What are you asking me Sam?"

"Well Stuart, you said the sign said free cookies so I want to know if they were chocolate chip cookies?"

Frank just shook his head again, "Come on Sam, this was a story that Stuart made up to explain in his own way what he knew he had to do. That's an analogy."

Sam could not let it go, "So there were no cookies?"

Carrie was mystified by Sam's words, "Give it a rest Sam, Stuart is going to help us and that is all that matters."

With joy in his voice, Frank added, "And Stuart, thank you and it's time for us to take you to the zoo to meet our friends."

"Sounds good Frank, you seem to be the leader so lead on, I will follow you."

This was such a strange trio and even though I knew that animals really don't talk, I was here for the ride and went with the flow. I just didn't know where this flow would take me.

Frank was definitely the leader of the trio and as we left the gazebo and into the plush green garden he said, "Just relax Stuart, everything will all be fine."

No way! Yea, no way that greenie knew what I was thinking but the way this whole day was going, anything was possible. "You know Frank, our walk to the zoo is like, well try this analogy out for size; it is like being buckled up on a rollercoaster ride and approaching the top and not knowing what's on the other side other than a quick and furious ride down."

"I get that Stuart but inside the park is the zoo, only a matter of a few more minutes. Well, maybe longer since Sam and Carrie are so very very slow."

I nodded and acknowledged Frank's comment, "Alright my friend, I'll be patient."

So we walked and walked and walked and finally reached the zoo and even at first glance, this was not like any other zoo I had ever seen. Three things that hit me right away were how clean it was, the animals were free to roam about and how I felt that I was truly immersed in their home. Oh yes, that wonderful aroma that only animals could appreciate; for me it just stunk.

Carrie piped in, "Doesn't it smell great?"

Sam added, "It sure does."

I looked down to Frank and I swear this crazy frog seemed to be smiling. He then said, "Come on Stuart, we are headed over to the zebras."

"And why Frank?"

Sam interjected, "Be like me Stuart, just keep moving on, just like me."

"So Sam, you want me to move at a snail's pace?"

Carrie added, "Come on boys, let's just all play nice; we have a mission to do and we know why Frank is taking us to the home of the zebras."

I was wondering why, "Thanks Carrie, but maybe the three of you know but I don't, so come on Frank spill the beans."

Sam spoke out, "You know Stuart, and you really have a thing about food. First it was the chocolate chip cookies and now you want beans?"

Carrie added, "Yea, good point Sam. So tell us what kind of beans?"

Sam replied, "Good follow-up question Carrie. So answer her Stuart."

Frank interrupted, "Don't answer that Stuart, I'll do it for you. Spilling the beans is an expression that simply is saying that someone's secret is going to be disclosed. Make sense to you Sam?"

"I get it Frank. What about you Carrie?"

"No, I still don't understand and why is Stuart going to take off his clothes?"

Frank shook his head in utter disbelief. "No Carrie, he is not taking his clothes off. Spilling the beans is a saying that someone uses when providing a secret they have to someone else. In other words, they are letting others know what their hidden secret is."

"I think I got it Frank but I still want to know about why Stuart is taking his clothes off?"

I could tell that Frank was so over Carrie's question so I knew that I should clarify what he said. "So Carrie, what Frank was trying to say was someone's secret is going to be disclosed which has nothing to do with clothes, just to reveal or uncover a secret and…"

Frank interrupted me, "Best to drop it Stuart. You got it now Carrie?"

Carrie nodded and Frank continued, "Good Carrie. Now let's all keep quiet and head to the zebra's, Zoey is waiting."

The Elevator

I stopped dead in my tracks, "Frank, who is Zoey?"

"Zoey is our one and only female zebra and she is so close to having her foal and that is where you come in."

"What is foul about her, please explain Frank?"

"Not foul, I said foal and just wait, we are almost at the home of our seven zebras; you'll know what is going on right away. Please Stuart, just chill; only a short distance remains to their home."

I did what I was asked to do and that was chill and minutes later, I saw the first of zebras. I counted them and there were six. I then asked Frank, "Now what, we are here and there are six zebras, not seven. What am I supposed to be looking at?"

No reply from Frank; we just continued to walk into an open area where the zebras were and then with a concerned voice he spoke out, "Look over to your right Stuart; Zoey is lying on the ground and she needs your help."

Frank, Sam and Carrie stood still and I slowly walked over to Zoey and saw what was going on; she was having her baby but it wasn't coming out.

With a concerned tone, Frank continued, "Come on Stuart, please help Zoey deliver her baby, we are afraid both will die without your help."

"But Frank, I don't know what to do, I'm just a kid and that's it."

Frank yelled back, "Never say just Stuart. Just a kid sounds like you making yourself something less than what you actually are. You are a kid and a good kid with lots of good qualities. Sam, help me convince Stuart that he can do it."

"Yea Stuart, you are a good kid that will help pull the baby out of Zoey."

Carrie added, "You can do it Stuart, I know you can do it."

Stumbling over my own words, "I appreciate what you are all saying but I have no idea what to do, I might do something to hurt either the baby or Zoey."

"But Stuart, if you do nothing, then both might die. Isn't that a good enough reason to help?"

"Yes Frank but what if…"

Sam interrupted, "No what if. Just get over there and help them both; now move!"

The Elevator

With all of their encouragement, I knew what I had to do; I took a deep breath and cautiously walked over to Zoey. I patted her on her swollen belly and told her that she would be fine. I then moved behind her and the baby was only part way out and I could see that the legs were turned in such a way that was blocking it from being pushed out. I reached in and felt around and somehow, someway I felt good enough at what I was doing and as I kept moving my hands around, I felt the baby zebra move. I slowly pulled my hands out and as I did the baby started moving. I moved further away from Zoey and watched in amazement as her baby was now being pushed out.

My new three friends yelled out in praise of what I did and how Zoey and her baby would be fine. I was quite proud of myself, "Now what, what do we next?"

Frank replied without hesitation, "Time to go back to the gazebo, your work is done here and we appreciate you and will never forget what you did. You are a wonderful human being Stuart."

I had tears in my eyes and even though there were words I wanted to say, I was so choked up that I was silent. Then, all around I heard many more animals making sounds and it was deafening; elephants, tigers, hippos, birds, lions, bears, giraffes and you name it, they were all around us.

Frank had so much joy in his voice, "That's all for you Stuart, they are expressing their appreciation like we just did. Helping one animal is like helping all of us. They don't talk like the three of us however; their sounds speak more volumes than we who voices can possibly say."

Carrie added, "That was perfect Frank; now let's get Stuart back to the gazebo."

The four of us left the zoo and it was time to go back to the gazebo; I took one last look back at Zoey and her baby and was shocked to see that it was already standing up and next to her mother.

No words were spoken as we made the journey to the gazebo and once there, we all sat down on the tiled floor. This was such a cool thing, Frank, Sam and Carrie were by my side and we shared our goodbyes as well as very kind and considerate words. I felt a special kind of friendship to my new friends and their words of appreciation touched my heart. This whole crazy thing that was going on was rather special, how three talking animals were able to bring a large degree of happiness into my soul was rather, well extraordinary. I had one last thing to say, "You know, meeting the three of you was as wonderful as having a peanut butter and jelly sandwich along with milk right before bedtime."

The three of them seemed to smile; Carrie piped in, "That was a cool analogy Stuart and speaking on behalf of Frank and Sam, we agree that meeting you was quite wonderful as well."

Frank sighed, "I couldn't have said it any better Carrie. You know Stuart; it always makes you feel good when you do the right thing. Think about the watch and charm bracelet and bye bye."

I stood up and before I could say anything else, the three of them had left and I felt a bit sad that the time we spent together had come to an end. What an amazing journey we shared. I looked around and saw them making their way back into the plush green grass and then I assumed they would go back to the zoo.

As I was thinking about all that happened, I finally got it; foal was the actual name for a baby zebra. After coming to this realization, I left the gazebo and headed back to the elevator; I played back in my head over and over again what Frank said to me about doing the right thing.

"Is that you Stuart?"

"Shake him, he seems asleep."

"I'm not going to put my hands on a total stranger, you do it Flanigan."

"Alright Josh, but why not you?"

"Look, I am a new Customer Service Rep and you are the boss; you shake him."

"Come on Stuart, wake up; your friend JJ found me and told me that you were stuck in the elevator. We rushed over here so come on, wake up."

I moaned and put my hand to my forehead, "What happened, where am I?"

"Remember me; I welcomed you and your friend to the store."

I looked up, "Yea, you are Frank, Frank Flanigan, right?"
"That's right and JJ is waiting downstairs to meet up with you. Can you stand up?"

I looked up to Flanigan and this other guy, "I am so confused; I remember the burning smell in the elevator as it was moving up; all of a sudden it came to stop and jolted me forward. I think I lost my balance and must have hit my head."

Frank Flanigan laughed out, "You think so?"

"But where am I?"

"You are outside the elevator on floor three."

I started to stand up and Flanigan and this other guy helped me to my feet. We then made our way to the elevator and right in front of me was my jacket. I quickly grabbed it and immediately reached into the pocket where JJ placed the stolen items; the watch and charm bracelet were there. We continued to walk a few more steps and I was first into the waiting elevator and stood silently in the back while Flanigan and the other guy were at the front. Don't know who pressed the button to close the doors but they sure closed quite quickly and we were headed down. The smell of the grinding motor was quite strong as we moved from the third floor to the second and then down toward floor one.

The elevator seemed to drop the final few feet to the first floor and the doors on the opposite side opened up. Frank and this other guy went out as I was putting on my jacket; once on I took a couple of steps forward. The doors abruptly started to close, I tried to stick my hand out to force them back open but it didn't work. The elevator began to move; I looked at the floor indicator above the doors and it moved from one to two then to three and it stopped with a loud thump on floor four.

The doors to the rear opened and upon exiting, my eyes were fixated on one of the most beautiful scenery sites I had ever seen. Sure, I had my fair share of traveling with my parents and also during school trips. Most were in the southwest and it would be hard to say that anyone spot was better than another however; I have always been partial to driving anywhere where large trees grew, like evergreens growing in abundance. So, right in front of me was this site, it was a forest just a matter of feet from where I was standing. So strange this day has been but now, I can just turn off my brain, walk into the forest and smell the wonderful fresh aroma; a wonderful smell like no other place.

I was glad that I had my jacket on as it was a bit chilly. I zipped it up all the way to the top and walked to the edge of the forest and then slowly walked in. I looked up and felt that my smile was so huge, like from one ear to the other; I was in heaven. Step by step, the trees were getting taller and taller. First, they were around my height, five foot five but then they were taller than me by inches and then feet and then it was like the sky was the limit.

The blue sky was the deepest blue I had ever seen and I wish I had the means to take a picture. I stopped and looked in every direction and had a prayer that I would remember this moment for the rest of my life. So special, so spectacular and such a life changing time for me; now if I only knew what this all meant. I could not even understand what the deal was with the ocean and the events that happened there. Then there were those crazy birds, the animals and now this, where and how does it all relate? It's like a piece of a puzzle that I want to get it to fit but right now, I didn't know how.

Off in the distance, a loud noise filled the still air and then another and another; it sounded like gunshots. A woman's shrill voice yelled out once and then again and again. Yet another shot, another and one more blood curdling scream and then there was silence. Nothing, no gunshots and no screaming; it was so strange and I had no idea what to do other than to trust my feelings and walk toward where the commotion had come from.

I was getting confused as I walked further into the forest and had the feeling that I was walking in circles; in addition, I was losing my breath. Was this search for the unknown gunshots and screaming worth it or would it be best to go back and give up on this journey to who knows where? I thought what was the point to walk in a forest, even though it looked and smelled so amazing? I was looking for something that seems to be; well the analogy is simple, like a pin in a haystack.

Despite all the questions I had bouncing around in my head, I still was compelled to find out what happened, what was the noise all about. I determined right at that moment that despite the lack of breath I was encountering or the courage I lacked or whatever I would face, nothing would keep me from finding out what I heard. I had a mission and that was to go forward and no turning back till I reached my goal even though at this time I didn't know what it was. I knew that I had to keep going and not give up no matter what. I stopped, closed my eyes and took in a deep breath of the wonderful fresh air and upon exhaling, I felt a bit more relaxed. I took the next couple of minutes to continue with the deep breathing and exhaling and this helped so much and then I felt fine.

My mind seemed to be cleared up and I decided not to rush, I would take my time and not let my emotions take over. My mission was simple, I had to find out what the screaming gal was all about; I had the worst feeling inside and knew it would not go away till I found her. I prayed that whatever was going on that there would be good news and not… I quickly dispelled this thought from my mind that something bad might have happened and replaced it with thinking that all would be just fine.

I began to slowly move forward and then again, a single gunshot and a woman's voice yelled out, "Right here, hurry!"

I felt energized and my steps picked up, I now knew deep down that I was on the correct path and then the voice once again filled the air, "We need you here!"

I turned to my right and felt I knew the direction the voice was coming from and began to run; I now had the feeling that not one but two or maybe three women needed help. I yelled out, "I'm on my way, help me find you, continue to talk to me!"

Someone heard me and replied, "Come on over."

The voice was louder so I knew I was headed in the correct direction. I continued and then the flat terrain of the forest changed, it was now a gradual incline and my running changed to a fast walk. I then lost my breath and had to stop; I bent over and rested with my hands on my knees and tried to calm down. I looked ahead, the hill before me looked daunting and no way could I make it up to the top in the condition I was in. I waited and it was a good five minutes later that I was ready to conquer the hill.

Urgency, yes this is what I was feeling as I started up the hill. Even though it was difficult to move fast, I tried my best knowing that I had to get to the top and whatever was going on, I knew I would find it. The big question was, what was it, what was I expecting to find?

Then, it was odd, no loud noises and no screams; I was now close to the top of the hill and then after a deep breath and a couple more feet to cover, I reached my goal. I was at the top of the hill and looked down into the valley and my eyes filled up with tears. My heart sank into my chest and felt a feeling that I last felt when I turned thirteen. You talk about a wow moment, this was a wowzie wowzie wow moment and my light tears turned into a full bucket of big baby tears. Best analogy to describe my tears would be they were like a baby that just dirtied their diaper and also was hungry and yellin' and yellin' out needing the mommy or daddy to clean and feed him or her, whichever the case may be. I dropped to the ground and placed my hands over my eyes and the tears, well they were flowing like a raging river.

I gazed down into the valley and finally the tears gave way to a smile, a rather large one in fact. Only this wonderful site could bring about such opposite emotions in me and in such a short time. I dried the tears from my eyes and cheeks; standing up I took a deep breath and knew that I had to complete my mission and that was to make it down the hill. I had to summon the courage from deep within to deal with thoughts that were so deeply embedded in my mind and heart.

It seemed like only yesterday when Becca and I were at the carnival; you know the ones that go from town to town and for a week or two. This one particular carnival was here and this was the fourth year in a row; it went up one week before spring break in my junior year of High School. I was quite happy the carnival was here; the first year in town was back when I was thirteen. Anyway, when I saw Becca for the first time, she was this seventeen-year-old amazingly cute girl, a senior, Class President and last year she was our school's Homecoming Queen. I had such a crush on her but my guess was that she would never ever ever ever say hello to me. She was actually the first girl that I liked and met her on the first day of school; I was sixteen, turning seventeen toward the end of the school year. Anyway, my guess was that she didn't even remember meeting me while in line at the class registration table. I even thought at the time that there would never be a time that a senior girl like her would ever talk to a guy like me, especially since I was a junior.

Becca seemed to be so cool and so much nicer than my guy friends. She had long brown hair down to her shoulders and a smile that was as bright as the morning sun; she was nothing like JJ or any of my guy friends. I quickly came to the realization that when laying things out, you know, boys versus girls, I felt that hanging out with such a cute girl would have so much more of an upside compared to the time hanging out with guys. There was only one problem; this was a dream that I wished would come true. Whenever I saw Becca, I was like a, well the analogy would be a new puppy that got separated from the mother and had such a sad face. Anyway, this is how I felt.

About five months later into the school year my dream came true, Becca and I met again at a basketball game and as crazy as it sounds, we started to hang out together before and after school. This went on for about a month and then things got even better, we started to meet up and walk together to our classes. About two weeks after this, things progressed and I would meet her after her Science Class and we would have lunch together in the cafeteria. It was so cool, I could tell that there were guys checking us out; who would have guessed that me, yes me would be sitting next to the hottest and coolest girl in school! I just knew there were guys that were jealous that I was with Becca and they were not with her. I also sensed there were girls that I knew from my classes that were looking at us; in my mind I had all these crazy thoughts that they wished they were the ones having lunch with me. Oh well, nothing like having these thoughts running around my head; all that mattered was that I was with Becca.

The real special day happened a few weeks after we started having lunch together; I ran into Becca in the hallway, she reached out for my hand and we walked together. This was only for a short distance as my next class was down the hallway and around the corner. Holding hands with her was very amazing and something totally new to happen to me; to say the least, I was like a new man, or at least a new teenage boy. I didn't really have any idea of what or how I should act with a girl but it was so much cooler than anything I experienced hanging out with the guys. Our walking together between classes was now even better than before as our hands were always tightly interlocked.

Our friendship grew over the months and it eventually led to our first kiss. Yea, I kissed an older woman, I mean an older girl; only one year older but still, it was the best thing that had ever happened to me. I felt like I was on top of the world; I knew that other guys were jealous, after all, Becca was like the best looking girl in school and we were inseparable throughout the school year.

Becca was special to me; so mature, so cute and she helped me to find the confidence in myself that I had yet to discover. Meeting her was the best thing that could have happened to me during the school year and I felt so very lucky that we found one another.

It was during spring break of that year that Becca and her family took off for a short four-day vacation and when she returned, we were only a week away from heading back to school. We took full advantage of this time to hang out together including going to the mall, going to a couple of movies and we had two full days to enjoy the carnival. It was the last two days the carnival would be in town; this was when it happened.

Becca and I were on the ride called Tilt Your Town, a cool ride with these round cars that held up to six people. These cars would turn in a circle one way and then turn the other way. The ride also had a rather neat feature as it would tilt up to a 45 degree angle and the cars turned at the same time; totally awesome! The backdrop of the ride resembled the city in which the ride was in and the ride was named after the tilt and the city backdrop.

This one particular time that we were on the ride and it must have been our fourth time over the weekend, there was something going on with this boy and girl that were in the car in front of us, they were yelling back and forth and it got so bad that the attendant running the ride stopped it. When it gradually stopped moving and was back down from being up at the angle, he told the two kids that they needed to leave and he escorted them off; just not me and Becca, others clapped and cheered as the ride resumed. It took only Becca and me a matter of seconds to get back into our nice embrace as the cars started to spin and then the tilt started.

Suddenly it stopped and an announcement was made that there was a mechanical problem and we had to leave at once. It was rough as the ride was on an angle and I held Becca's hand tightly as we carefully made our way out of the car we were in and down toward the exit ramp. A young boy and girl maybe only eight were in front of us and they were having a hard time walking from their car and then the girl fell. She screamed out and because of the tilt, she began to roll down and I could tell that she was going to either hit one of the stranded cars or the side railing. No one did anything but I let go of Becca's hand but only after telling her to stay put and hold onto one of the support beams. Without thinking twice, I ran as fast as I could to catch up with this girl who was rolling down the ride; it was so hard running between the cars and the tilt sure didn't help but I knew I had to get to this girl before she was injured. Just then, the ride started up but for only a few seconds and then it came to a sudden stop. I was hit by a moving car and it pushed me down but this didn't deter me, I got up and ran like crazy and reached the girl just before she was hit by one of the cars. I picked her up and looked behind me, Becca was right there and reached out and grabbed the back of my shirt to keep me balanced. The three of us were able to get to the exit of the ride and then still carrying the girl, we made it down the stairs.

A woman yelled out to us and then grabbed the girl from my arms. Frantically she screamed out, "Thank You, Thank You so much for saving my daughter!"

I looked over at this woman holding her daughter so tightly and with my heart pounding and totally out of breath, "I only did what I had to do."
She replied, "Thank You so much, you are a special boy and you saved my daughter's life."

I was going to say something but the mother and her daughter walked away and I stood there, breathing so fast and then Becca, well she looked at me and her beautiful green eyes and my eyes connected and we kissed. I truly believe that one kiss was beyond any of the other kisses we shared and felt that I was in love for the first time and was the happiest boy in the whole world.

Now, looking down from the top of the hill, a rather large carnival was in the valley and I was so anxious to go down to it. My thoughts about what happened during spring break with me and Becca and the girl that fell were still dancing around in my head. In addition to that, I thought back to how so much changed over the final month of the school year.

Becca and I hung out together for so much of that later part of the year but, I found out that no matter what and how much I wanted more to happen, she had her own plan and having me being a part of it was not in the cards. Yes, there were times that I believed that she was not interested in anyone other than me. One huge problem, a few weeks after spring break and the event that happened at the carnival, the first huge crush in my life came to a crashing end.

Becca met me after my last class of the day and it was a Monday. She gave me a kiss on the cheek and simply said it was cool knowing me but that it was time to move on. She sure did and I was so messed up as I left school but as I walked home, I felt better that I had her in my life even for the last part of the year. After all, my first kiss was with her and that was something I will always hold onto. Now, I had to make it down the hill, corn dogs, caramel apples, and snow cones would be waiting for me. The loud noises that I heard as I made my way through the forest were of course the magical sounds that one would hear coming from a carnival.

The Elevator

I started down the hill but something inside said to stop and go back to the elevator; I had to get back to the store and rid myself of the guilt that I was now feeling for being part of the stealing of the watch and charm bracelet. I reached into the pocket in the jacket and was relieved to know that I didn't lose the items through this odd but yet happy journey. Now, I knew it was time to do the right thing, return the items to the Customer Service Rep, Frank Flanigan. It was a long walk and finally, I was back at the beginning of the forest and the elevator was right in front of me and the doors were open. I turned around and took one last look at the forest and my journey to the top of the hill. I had fond memories about the carnival and of course Becca. Now, I was ready to move forward and that was going into the elevator and down to the first floor. Time to fess up for what I did.

I walked in and the doors closed and I pushed the button for the first floor but it didn't light up. I pushed it again and again, still no light and then finally it started to move. I was ready to put this day behind me and returning what JJ had stolen and gave to me was the right thing to do; convincing JJ of this might just be another story in itself. Regardless, I was going to do the right thing.

Time seemed to be standing still as the elevator made it slowly down to the third floor and then floor two and then it stopped. The lights in the elevator went dark and I stood alone and my thoughts reflected upon all that happened on this rather weird afternoon. One thing for sure, I was going to do the right thing once the elevator reaches the first floor but the problem was when would it move? I pushed the open door button but nothing happened. I pushed the button to go back up to the third floor but nothing happened other than I began to freak out over my stranded situation; why me? What was going on and was there a reason that I had such weird things happen from the time JJ and I entered the elevator after the taking of the items? I pushed the help button but no response and I threw my hands up in the air and yelled out, "Why me?"

All of a sudden, a woman's voice came through the speaker, "You have a problem?"

I laughed and replied, "Well, yes. The lights went out in here and I am stuck on the second floor."

"Did you push any buttons other than help?"

I was instantly frustrated with this woman and with a tinge of sarcasm; "I know how to push the button to the floor I want to go to, so get this thing moving!"

"And what floor did you push?"

I yelled out, "One, I pushed one!"

"Are you in elevator number three?"

The Elevator

It was hard to see in the dark but there was just enough light for me to see the gold-plated number three that was right above the floor panel. "Yes, I am in elevator three."

"Well, that explains why you are stuck on floor two."

"Great, so why?"

"Well, there were kids playing in the elevator earlier and we had reports to check to see what if anything they did."

"Alright, so did they?"

"Did they what?"

I was getting perturbed, "Well, apparently they did something but no idea what that might have been."

"Nor am I but stay put, I will turn on the override lights for you."

Like I had no choice other to stay put so I politely replied, "Thank You."

A couple of lights came on, "The lights are on, now what?"

"Try pushing the first floor button again and tell me what happens."

"Alright, I am pushing the button but nothing, nothing is happening."

"Is the floor indicator to the side of the actual button to the first floor to the left or right of the two?"

I was confused, "To what?"

"No, not that to, two as in the number."

I felt rather dumb, "Oh, I get what you are saying; the floor indicator button for floor two is to the left of the one."

"Which one sir?"

This was crazy but I had nothing else to do other than keep my cool and with a deep breath and a good exhale, "The indicator to floor one is to the right of floor two."

The woman laughed, "Kids, nothing other than the kids that we caught playing around in that elevator. Please sir, push the button for floor two and tell me what happens."

I did as instructed, "The elevator is moving, it's moving!"

The Elevator

"Great sir, the kids probably were being kids and put something over the indicators to confuse people and I guess they accomplished their devilish trick."

I barked back, "You think?"

I looked at the buttons and sure enough, there was paper taped over the indicators for floor one and two. "I see what they did and I am now back on floor one."

"Good sir, have a great day and thank you for shopping at…"

I interrupted her, "The door is not opening, any idea why?"

"Well sir, why not try pushing the close door button."

"If you say so, I will do it." I pushed the button and the doors opened, "Thank you, whoever you are."

"You are welcome and it all came down to kids being kids and horsing around after school let out for the summer; kids can be crazy at times and forget how their actions, even as simple as they believe they are, can affect others and the effect could in turn hurt not only themselves but others. Enjoy your shopping!"

Great, a lecture and it wasn't even from a teacher in school however, these might have been the best words I heard and they sunk deep down into my life. I left the elevator and JJ was sitting down on a bench to the side of the elevator. I shook my head and walked over to him and without hesitation I said, "Let's do the right thing and return the items that we took."

Without hesitation JJ replied, "Yea Stuart, you are right, it was a crazy thing for me to do; not a cool thing at all."

So, JJ and I walked to the counter where the items were swiped from and we ran into the Customer Service Rep, Frank Flanigan; we pulled out the watches and charm bracelets and handed them over to him.

I did the talking, "Sorry sir, we were both acting like big shot grown up kids and dumb, yea we were acting really dumb."

He glared at us and we both knew that something bad was going to come our way; he called over the sales clerk and handed the items to her.

Flanigan went on to explain to the clerk, "Since the boys didn't leave the store and that they pleaded stupidity, we will let them off."

We then casually walked out of the store and back into the mall.

"By the way Stuart, what took you so long to get out of the elevator?"

I smiled as I looked at JJ, "Let's just say that it was an adventure and lessons that I needed to learn were learned. It's time now to enjoy our summer break."

"That's all you have to say, none of your crazy analogies?"

"Nope JJ, nothing more to say."

My Second Short

You Must Be Kidding Me

You Must Be Kidding Me

Happy New Year to all my dear friends, I love you all so dearly. That is what I said right at the stroke of midnight just four months ago. Little did I know that shortly after my words that came from deep within my life, one of my friends in attendance disappeared and has not been seen since. To this day, I have many wonderful thoughts about Crystal. Crystal is as sparkling of a person as crystal sold in any high-end department store; you know like glasses, serving plates and of course jewelry ranging from rings to necklaces. Crystal is a gem like no other and I wish I knew what happened to her.

I was questioned at home about her disappearance on the Monday following the New Year's Eve party; I was given New Year's Day off. There was a knock at my front door and it was at three in the afternoon; I was hesitant to even open the door. I looked out to the front door from the side room and it was a woman with a badge in her hand; knowing that this was an officer of the law, I opened the door and said, "Good afternoon officer."

The officer on the other side of the screen took out her identification, "Sorry to bother you, I am Detective Lenah Lockheart and I would like to talk to you."

To say the least, I was quite taken by this and replied, "Okay, how may I help you?" I am sure that she heard the nervousness in my voice.

You Must Be Kidding Me

"Relax Mr. Brewstard; I am following up on a reported missing person from Brissell's Department Store."

"Sorry to interrupt, the T is silent."

"What T?"

"The T in my name. It is pronounced as Brewsard."

"Alright Mr. Brewstard."

I wanted to correct her for pronouncing my name with the T but decided it best to let it go. "Please just call me Rob and how do you know my name?"

"Let's just say that I know all that I need to know about you but I do need to know more. May I now come into your house sir?"

"Please come in detective." I opened the screen door and welcomed her in and pointed to the leather chair next to my couch. "Please have a seat detective."

Whatever was going on here felt so odd and all sorts of things started running through my head.

The detective continued, "I need to confirm a few things for my records."

You Must Be Kidding Me

"Go ahead."

"I see that you are a male of 35 years of age and you are currently living here at 39051 Bridgewater Court, and you were born in Wichita Kansas. You are single and have never been married. You have been working at Brissell's Department Store for ten years."

"Well detective, you have done your homework; I am curious why you are here and know so much about me?"

With a deadpan look and a most serious voice she replied, "Just doing my job sir. Now, let's start with what you can tell me about Crystal."

I responded, "What kind of crystal?"

"Crystal at Brissell's."

"Well detective, I first worked in the department about one year before my promotion to Sales Manager over Menswear. It was a little over three months ago that I was named the Store Sales Director and still kept my position of Sales Manager; we are actively looking to fill this position. While working in the China Department, we carried crystal glasses, plates, serving trays and many other beautiful items."

You Must Be Kidding Me

"I am not talking about crystal as in objects Mr. Brewstard; I am here to know about Crystal Champion."

"Why didn't you say so? Is there something particular you want to know?

"Well Mr. Brewstard..."

I was getting a bit exasperated with her, "Sorry detective, please no T."

"That's right, I do not want any."

"Want any what?"

"Tea, I don't want any."

"Not that tea, the T in my last name is silent and what do you want to know about Crystal?"

"Sorry sir, what was your association with her a few days prior to New Year's Eve?"

"Once again, please call me Rob."

"Okay and you can call me Lenah."

"That might be hard for me to do, I have deep respect for our law enforcement and calling you by your first name and not last name is odd and ..."

You Must Be Kidding Me

She interrupted me, "It's alright, I want you to feel comfortable and prefer for you to relax and call me Lenah."

What was I going to say to her other than what she asked and with a more relaxed voice I questioned her, "Well Detective Alright, what do you want to know?"

"Please, you can call me Lenah."

I hesitated, "Okay Detective Lenah Alright."

"It's Lockhart, not Alright."

"Anything I can do to help you, are you not feeling okay?"

"I am fine Rob, let me continue. I am working on the case of a missing woman by the name of Crystal, Crystal Champion. Her family called police headquarters right after midnight to report her as missing; it was indicated in the report that she should have been home no later than ten and that this was most unusual that she didn't come home nor call. After arriving this morning to work, I was given the report and checked with her employer and they had yet to see her. I spoke to her family, friends and work colleagues and no one has any information to share. One common thing that her co-workers said was to talk to you, not sure why but that is why I am here. I am trying to put together all the pieces that led up to your New Year's Eve party last night and maybe there might be something that leads me to anything, anything at all."

"Well Detective Lockheart..."

I was interrupted, "You have my last name correct but please call me Lenah, alright Rob?"

"Alright Lenah."

There was dead silence that seemed to last forever and then Lenah said, "I'm waiting Rob?"

"On what?"

"What can you tell me about you and Crystal? Did you see her prior to the party?"

"Over the years I worked with her but in different departments however, I didn't see her at all the week prior to New Year's Eve."

"What was your work relationship with her?"

With a very inquisitive voice I replied, "Are you asking me if we had a relationship?"

"Relax Rob, what I meant was what was your working relationship, you know day to day work?"

You Must Be Kidding Me

I felt more relaxed once she clarified her question, "I saw her a few days before Christmas in the line at the coffee shop right next door to our store."

"You both work at Brissell's, right?"

"I thought that was already established but yes, I am the Sales Manager in Menswear and Crystal was in China prior to moving into my department."

"And how long was she in China?"

"Not sure but for at least six months."

"Isn't that a long time to be there?"

"No, not really, most employees move between departments and stay there for a year or more. We have great loyal employees who are dedicated and stay with the managers they really like working for."

"Okay, now I understand. So, she was in China, not the country, the department, right Rob?"

"Why on earth did you think that, of course, the China Department and prior to that she was in the Houseware Department?"

"Sorry, I misunderstood you. So she moved from the China Department and worked with you in Menswear."

You Must Be Kidding Me

"Yes, she was working with me."

"You said was, what exactly did you mean by was? Would you like to explain that?"

"I was her manager till early December and that is when she left my sales team and moved over to Marketing. I didn't see her at work; my office was on the first floor and Marketing was on the second floor behind the furniture."

"So she worked behind the Furniture Department?"

I was wondering at this point if I was speaking a different language to Lenah; well the office she worked in was actually down the hall a bit from the Furniture Department but yes, she worked behind the furniture."

I sensed Lenah was confused, "Let me be more specific. There is a small lobby area in front of the offices and Marketing is directly behind the furniture."

"Okay, now I get it and I have a good picture in my head where she worked. Please clarify; did you see Crystal in line to get coffee?"

"Yes, as I said that was the last time I saw her."

"So Rob, what did you do?"

You Must Be Kidding Me

"Well, I ordered."

"And what did you order?"

"Coffee."

"Plain or with something else like mocha or hazelnut?"

"I drink my coffee plain, but I do add cream and sugar."

"What else did you do?"

"I sat down with Crystal and we had a nice talk about her new job."

"Did you have anything else or did you talk about anything that one would consider being out of the ordinary?"

"I did ask for sugar and I had a chocolate double chip cookie."

"And is Sugar a waitress at the coffee shop?"

Once again, this detective and I were not on the same page and at that moment, I decided to play her game. "She must have been off that day."

"Why do you say that Rob?"

You Must Be Kidding Me

"Because Sugar never came to my table."

"So that's why you assume she wasn't there, correct?"

"Yes Lenah, that is correct."

"What about the cookie, the chocolate chip cookie."

"It was a double."

"A double what Rob."

"Chocolate chip, I ordered a double chocolate chip cookie."

"Did you get it?"

I was so finished with this crazy conversation but after taking a deep breath, I answered, "Yes, I had the cookie; now can we get back to Crystal, please?"

"That's fine. Did anything happen between you and Crystal?"

"Nothing... oh yes, I remember we talked about the destruction of the rainforest and global warming. We also talked about the rights of all..."

You Must Be Kidding Me

"Sorry to break in, did you sense anything odd about Crystal, anything that might help in our search for her?"

"No, nothing that I can think of plus we only had no more than five minutes to talk. I had a meeting to rush off to and Crystal had to leave as well. She told me she had to rush back to work for an appointment."

"What kind of meeting Rob?"

"It was our managers meeting with our store Manager Ashley Kood."

"Not your meeting, what about Crystal's meeting?"

"Don't know, I didn't ask as I was rushing off to meet with Ms. Kood."

"So Ms. Ashley could tell me? Is it possible to call her now?"

"No no no Lenah, Ashley is her first name and Kood is her last name."

"Thank you for clearing that up. So could she tell me about the meeting she rushed off to?"

"She would not know anything about Crystal as she has a different manager."

You Must Be Kidding Me

"Fine but I would still like to talk to her; can you give me a number to call her or not?"

"Now you want Knot's number?"

Lenah had a dazed look and replied back, "Not who?"
"Emery Knot, head of Store Security."

"No, not Knot, but Kood, Ashley Kood."

"That's fine Lenah; you want it so you can ask her about the meeting that Crystal was headed off to right?"

"Yes that's right, so please may I have the number?"

"By the way it wasn't a meeting, it was an appointment."

"Does that really matter Rob? Either way you don't know where she was off to do you?"

"I guess not Lenah. So you want to ask Ashley if she knew about the appointment Crystal was going to because I don't know?"

"Sounds like you don't want to get the number for me; are you refusing to get it Mr. Brewstard?"

You Must Be Kidding Me

I took yet another deep breath, "I did not know then and do not know now what appointment Crystal was headed off to. There is also no reason to check with our store manager as she does not micro manage the managers under neither her nor any of our employees; she trusts them to do their work and that is it."

"That's fine Rob so let's move on to the party on New Year's Eve. So clear your mind and let's get down to just this one period of time. All right with you?"

"Sure Lenah, just the evening of New Year's Eve."

I wasn't too sure where Lenah was going and felt a bit uncomfortable as we continued to talk. At least now, I was hopeful that something of substance might come up that will help her find Crystal. This was my hope but when the next question came out, my hopes were greatly diminished.

"Alright Rob, did you and Crystal engage in anything that would not really be things you would do at a company party?"

I was amused by Lenah's question and decided to play along. "Other than the massive amount of liquor and finding an open room where we could talk, nothing else that I can think of."

You Must Be Kidding Me

"Well, I can tell that you are just humoring me and I have only one other question for you."

Detective Lockheart was serious with her last question and I felt that I needed to show the respect that she deserved. "What is your question detective?"

With a somewhat monotone voice, "Do you have any idea what might have happened to Crystal? Any idea at all?"

"I wish I could help you. Crystal is an amazing woman and I hope that she didn't run into foul play. I would like for you to keep me informed about your investigation and I will have her in my prayers."

"Thank you. I will keep you abreast of any developments and hope it is good news. Have a great rest of the day and thank you for taking time for me."

She reached forward and I extended my hand, a nice handshake took place and she said, "It was a pleasure meeting you Mr. Brewstard."

"Nice meeting you as well Detective Lockheart and remember, the T is silent."

She chuckled, "Yes I know that and it was totally intentional and please, since I am so familiar with you and the missing report on Crystal, communicate with me and only me. We have such a huge caseload at headquarters and we are all working on our own cases."

"Alright Layla, I will talk only to you."

"That's Lenah, not Layla."

"I know; that was intentional as well."

We both laughed and I held the door for her as she set foot on the brick walkway; I closed the door and thoughts of Crystal ran through my head. I went over to a chair and then I closed my eyes and had a prayer for her. My prayer was simple, let Crystal be safe and sound and let no harm come her way.

January seemed to pass by like lightning and then before I knew it, the office Valentine's Day dinner and dance party was upon us. I was so into this event this year; I just knew that I would have the time of my life. I did have a couple of flashbacks to what happened to Crystal and it was odd that I didn't hear back from Detective Lockheart; guess that my statements were sufficient to show her that I didn't know anything about her disappearance. Strange, no one at work brought up anything about our Crystal Champion, so I decided it was time to let it go. Everyone at work is always so busy and we all concentrate on making today the best day at Brissell's.

You Must Be Kidding Me

I was part of the planning team for the Valentine's Day gala and from the onset knew that I would really need to let my ideas shine through as well as work harder than everybody else on the team. Just my luck, the head of Human Resources Ms. Rhonda May was on the team and I was not going to let her intimidate me as she had in the past and take over the planning. The best way to describe Ms. May is that she is very passionate about her job and a hard worker that wouldn't think twice about staying not one, not two but even three hours after the end of the normal workday. She is a workaholic and demands her employees to work as hard as she does.

I was quite fortunate when I received some great info from Pam Whaz, Rhonda May's Admin Assistance. She slipped with the info when we were casually talking about the upcoming planning meeting, she told me that Rhonda May had a different side to herself when she had one or two drinks. This sure was a good thing to know moving forward. Pam telling me this would be a huge help as the first planning meeting would be next Monday, the fourth and just twelve days till the big party. This newfound knowledge would help me through the planning and I felt good that I knew a little something about my perceived perfect Ms. Rhonda May. I felt more relaxed knowing whatever I may or may not do, Rhonda May may not be as tough on me as I may have first thought. So happy that Pam Whaz was there for me with this gem of information.

You Must Be Kidding Me

Rhonda and I started the week working rather well together planning all aspects of the party. We both had such a large workload and the planning added so much to our time, we quickly realized that we needed to bring someone else into our team and Pam Whaz was the logical choice. We put her in charge of the invitations and we knew that she would take care of this without any difficulties. In fact, Rhonda and Pam gradually left me out of the planning and this was really no big deal to me.

I hardly did much of anything leading up to the party with my main responsibility being the entertainment, decorations, and cleanup. Oh how exciting the cleanup sounded to me however, the entertainment and decorations were right up my alley. I had no doubt that I would find the best fun stuff for our Valentine's Day party at an adult party store and knew it would be best not to tell Rhonda May or Pam Whaz what I was planning and doing. My new motto in life was simple, it is better to be quiet and not tell what you are up to until things are over and then, who really gives a hoot how things did or didn't work out because things are finished and you really can't go back. Pretty long motto but it is something that I might stick to in life.

Anyway, I had a fun time shopping at the adult store and picked up items that I thought would be great for the party. Even though there were things that I enjoyed checking out, the items I purchased were all above the line, nothing that would raise an eyebrow if you know what I mean. I took the goodies home and they stayed there till the day of the party; sure didn't want anyone to see what I had in store for the hotel's ballroom where the party would be held.

I did all the prep work leading up to the party that I could do from work and even at home. The ballroom at the hotel that we rented would be available for me to decorate at one and I was there just as they opened the room. I solicited the help of two sales clerks, Cindy and Ryan to help decorate and I must say that the three of us did a great job in the ballroom. We had it decorated from top to bottom with the red hearts, red roses and cute silver cupids of various sizes, each hanging from the ceiling. Of course Rhonda and Pam would look at the cupids as being excessive but I thought the little devils were rather cute; after all what expresses love on Valentine's Day any better than cupid? The three of us left and we had the hotel staff lock the room; we would return an hour before the doors would open for our employees, their spouses or significant others. Being a Saturday, this was going to be a party that all in attendance would long remember.

About a week ago, I received word that Pam had sent out the invitations and included a message asking that all in attendance be dressed in their sexiest but modest form of dress to celebrate the day of love. I was confused by Pam's request and tried wrapping my head around how someone could dress sexy but modest? She left the door open to me and I didn't hold back as I arrived at the party wearing black pants with bright red tennis shoes. My fire engine red shirt which was designed to be worn over my pants, I guess they call it tails, had only three buttons at the bottom; the top was cut wide and the sides were laced with hot pink fabric. I liked the look and I did this not for me, but for the women of course.

I also had a hat that was red and black and in the shape of a box of chocolate candy. I must say, I looked great! I was strutting around the room welcoming all that entered and was so shocked to see the Kan sisters. I first met the twins about six years ago while working in Sporting Goods, Mary Kan was a Cashier and Carol Kan was a Sales Associate. When I saw them, let's just say that my eyes were focused on them and no one else in the room seemed to matter. They looked so amazing and I totally forgot that I was supposed to mingle with all the guests prior to being seated for dinner.

I got my act together and continued to mingle as most everyone was slowly finding a seat at the dinner tables. Well, I felt that my assigned duty was almost over so I worked my way over to the table where the sisters were seated. I approached them, almost in unison they jumped up and hugged me and I received a kiss from both. Wow, I was so happy, two beautiful women kissing me and Mary's hot pink lipstick was displayed for everyone to see on my right cheek and Carol's bright red lipstick was on my left cheek. Did I care about this, not at all and I was enjoying everyone focusing on the amazing Kan twins and me. Hard to describe the twins other than beyond sexy and what they were wearing totally complied with the request on the invitation. They were the best-dressed ladies, or maybe it would be best to say the best semi dressed ladies, if you know what I mean. Let's just say that all the men must have been so envious of me and did this bother me, no, not at all.

I felt that it was time for me to move on and greet the late arrivals so I excused myself from the twins and as I walked away from the table I was looking not forward but back to these two most beautiful women and clumsily tripped and landed on my rear. Most of the time I would have been embarrassed by this but now, I got off the floor and regained my composure and smiled at the sisters. They were chuckling and their smiles exposed their perfectly straight and bright white teeth. So, I continued to move on and of course who appeared to talk to me, yes Rhonda May and Pam Whaz. I was reminded that my main thing to do tonight, at least through dinner, was to be a host and not to just two but to everyone. Pam Whaz was the one who repeated that I was to be the host to everyone and I nodded and replied nicely and then went on to greet our fellow employees, spouses and their significant others, whomever they may be.

You Must Be Kidding Me

Dinner went off without a hitch and then the party began and there were lots and lots of hugging, dancing, and of course kissing. This was the day for lovers and the employees of Brissell's sure knew how to party. Being single, well this was a no brainer for me; a dance with Carol Kan and then I asked Mary Kan if she would like to dance and we hit the dance floor.

After the dance, Mary and I went back to the table where Carol was sitting and we all chilled and sat out the next dance. But after the next song, the twins and I hit the dance floor and I could not take my eyes off them nor could others as they watched the three of us dancing together. We then had time to catch up between dances, as it was over two years since we last saw each other. I didn't know that they had both been working at our sister store located across town and Mary told me that they moved and started at Brissell's just two weeks ago. To say the least, I was happy to know they were with us; nothing but the best at Brissell's and we had two of the best any employer would love to have. As for me, well I was so happy that they were back at the store and as the night wore one, we were getting so close and I do mean that in proximity as well as connecting from our hearts.

What a wonderful dinner and dance and I hated saying good night to the twins; I walked them to a waiting cab and we kissed. I promised them that tonight would be the first of many nights that we would get together. I waved as they drove off; I was sweating even though the temperature was a cool 50 degrees. I went back into the ballroom and sure enough, Pam and Rhonda were waiting for me and I thought I was going to get an earful from them however, I was thanked for putting together the most wonderful Valentine's Day dinner and dance in memory here at Brissell's.

The next morning, right at eleven, I received a call from our head of security, Emery Knot and he asked me to meet him in his office at one. I was rather puzzled why he would want to meet and I began throwing around crazy thoughts in my head; I figured it must have to do with the party, like a wrap up. Sure, that is what it must be, one of those meetings that we review what we did right and what we did wrong. So, I just went about working in the office, checked out what was going on in the department, had lunch and before I knew it, it was time to go to the meeting.

I met Knot and after sitting down, he began to tell me the reason for the meeting. He indicated that the twins did not report to work this morning and even Human Resources called them at home, however there was no answer. Emery went on to say that an employee who works in Security called the twins' family but nothing of substance was provided other than the twins were not seen since the time they left for the party the night before. Based on not knowing anything else said Knot, the family filed a missing person's report with the police earlier this morning.

I left Knot's office not knowing what was going on. I had the most horrible feeling that the report would bring back Detective Lenah Lockheart to question me about the missing persons and once again, from a company party. I was not happy and felt that Emery was not thrilled with yet another disappearance and this time not one person but two. I managed to get through the day with nothing-unusual happening and very pleased that I didn't hear anything else from Emery.

The next day and it was late in the morning, Emery called me to attend a meeting along with Rhonda and Pam; it was to be held in our boardroom along with a detective and at eleven. I had the dreaded feeling it was going to be Lenah and I didn't have any time to gather my thoughts, as it was a quarter till eleven when the call came in. I left my office and walked down the hall and turned down the next hallway only to be met at the elevator by Rhonda and Pam. No one spoke a word as we went up two floors to our administrator's boardroom. We were greeted at the door by Emery and inside the room, Lenah Lockheart was waiting.

I let the ladies in first and then walked over to Detective Lockhart and politely said, "Lenah, so nice to see you."

You Must Be Kidding Me

She reached out and we shook hands, she added, "And Rob, what can I say?"

Emery Knot spoke up, "Please everyone, take a seat and I would like to introduce Detective Lenah Lockheart and she is joining our meeting this morning. Others in attendance include Rob Brewstard and from HR we have Pam Whaz and Rhonda May and I am Emery Knot. I will now turn the meeting over to Detective Lockhart."

"First of all, thank you for coming to this meeting, please feel comfortable and call me Lenah. If you are wondering why I am here, I have been sent from our police headquarters to follow-up with the disappearance of Carol Kan and her sister Mary Kan. Can any of you tell me when you last saw them?"

Emery spoke up, "I believe that Rhonda May may be able to give you the best information."

Lenah responded, "Thank you Emery, and Rhonda for my records, what is your last name?"

"May."

"May what please?"

"Just May and I was at the dinner and party along with Rob and Pam was there as well."

You Must Be Kidding Me

"So, of the three of you, who had the most contact with the sisters?"

Rhonda quickly jumped in, "Oh by far Rob, he was rather chummy with them."

"Do you agree Pam"?

"Definitely, he was getting rather close to them and for that matter, the two of them were not doing anything to push him away. "

"May I say something detective?"

"Yes you may and your last name Pam is what?"

"No, it's Whaz, you might be thinking of Bonnie Whyt but to answer your question, Rob was hanging onto the Kan's like glue."

"Thank You Pam, but Bonnie who?"

"Not Bonnie Whoo, she lost him four years ago when he abruptly asked for a divorce; turned out he simply wanted to be single. Bonnie agreed to the divorce and was single until recently when she married a wonderful man, Walter Whyt."

'That is Walter what?"

"Yes Lenah, that's correct."

You Must Be Kidding Me

Lenah scratched her forehead and said, "For my records, please spell his full name."

Pam did what she was asked, "First name is W A L T E R and his last name is W H Y T, but when you say the last name, the Y is silent so even though it might look like White, it is pronounced as What."

With an inquisitive voice she questioned, "What?"

"Yes, that is accurate and Bonnie is very happy with Walter."

I had enough of the discussion and piped in, "Lenah, can we please talk about the main issue which is the disappearance of the twins?"

"Sure Rob but Pam was talking and I want her to finish what she was saying. So Pam, may I have the spelling of your last name?"

Pam was frustrated as well and you could hear it in her voice, "It is simple Detective Lockhart, my last name is Whaz, spelled W H A Z and I am the Admin Assistant to Rhonda May. Bonnie Whyt was previously married; her former husband's last name was Whoo. Bonnie is the Corporate Director over Finance. Rob, please get back to telling Detective Lockheart about the Kan sisters."

You Must Be Kidding Me

I cleared my throat once and then a second time, "Thank you Pam, I'll take it from here. So Lenah, as Pam said the girls and I were rather close to one another. Previously I worked with them here in the store and dated Mary for about six months and then when I asked her to be my girlfriend she dumped me!"

"And what happened next?"

"I was very sad, even close to having a bout of depression and this was all over the break up. One thing led to another and I started to date Carol."

Rhonda spoke up with a shrill voice; "You really went from one sister to the other sister? That's not cool Rob and ..."

Pam interrupted, "I agree, that was not a good thing to do and then to be working with them at the same store surely violates some policy. Does it not Knot?"

"Well ladies, I do not know of anything in our corporate policies that speaks about who can date whom and if the Kan sisters didn't complain then I don't have anything that I can say about Rob's behavior. We should pose this question to HR so Rhonda, does it?"

Rhonda replied, "Listen to what you are all saying, this dating of the twins was in the past, let's get to the present." There was quiet and then, "Rob, anything to say?"

"Yes, may I speak Lenah?"

"Please go ahead Rob. Ms. May and Whaz, and you too Knot, please let him finish and don't interrupt."

Rhonda added, "I agree, let's just move onto the Valentine's Day dinner and party, all right with you detective."

"Yes and go ahead Rob; that was going to be my suggestion."

"Thank you Lenah. I was so happy to see the twins and yes I was enamored by them in many ways. I danced with them and yes we had a little bit of kissing going on."

Pam Whaz was stunned by Rob's words, "Hardly a little kissing Rob, you three were over each other like hot chocolate fudge over a sundae."

"Please Ms. Whaz; let Rob tell us what was going on."

I continued, "As I was saying before being interrupted; I was getting, well let's say reacquainted with the twins and having them both at the same time was a pure treat."

You Must Be Kidding Me

Emery Knot raised his voice, "Come on Rob, and let's keep it…"

"Sorry Knot, I was saying that it was nice sitting with them and catching up on things and yes we might have been a bit too much into what we were doing and not Knot, using our best common sense."

"You think so Rob?"

"Yes Emery, we just got carried away and when the music started and went to the slow music, well I reached out for both of the sisters and we danced together."

Lenah questioned, "What else was going on Ms. Whaz while the Kan sisters and Rob danced?"

"Well I didn't see anything else Detective Lockheart."

"What about you Ms. May?"

"At first I was embarrassed watching the three of them dancing together but a few minutes later, I felt a deep sense of caring that they shared; to be truthful, it was rather sweet."

"That was it?"

"Yes Detective."

You Must Be Kidding Me

"Thank you Ms. Whaz."

Lenah wrote down some notes and then continued with her questioning, "Alright Rob, what happened at the end of the party? What was the last thing you did with the twins?"

"I walked them to a cab; kissed Carol and then Mary and wished them good night. That was it Lenah."

"Do you agree Ms. Whaz?"

"I really don't know as I was not there at the time."

"So you were Knot?"

"Once again Detective, no I was not there."

"Sorry Ms. Whaz, I was asking Emery."

He then replied, "What Lenah?"

Lenah carried on with her questioning, "Did you see anything out of the ordinary when Rob walked the twins to the cab?"

"Not I, I was watching over the whole room and not focusing on any particular thing. Besides, I was not outside, only inside."

You Must Be Kidding Me

"Thank you Knot and anything else from you Ms. Whaz?"

"Let me just say that I know Rob and if he said that he left them at the cab, then I believe him."

"Ms. May, is that a correct appraisal of what Pam said?"

"Yes Lenah."

Lenah looked at her notes, "Previously Pam, you did say if he said that…"

Pam interrupted, "I totally believe that Rob was telling the truth about what happened with Carol and Mary Kan and maybe Ms. May may have something to add."

"Ms. May, do you?"

"Nothing at all detective, I agree with what Pam said."

"Knot, anything from you."

"No, not a thing Lenah other than Rob is a good honest man and Pam, Rhonda and I have the utmost respect for him."

"Rob, anything to add?"

You Must Be Kidding Me

"Please Lenah, keep us all informed on what you find out about the Kan sisters."

Lenah replied, "Of course, I can and will keep you and the others informed about them." She then added, "Please contact me directly, I am taking care of this as well as the first missing person report, no need to talk to anyone else."

With that, we all left and just like the disappearance of Crystal, no idea what happened to the Kan sisters. Emery, Pam, Rhonda and I left the room as Lenah was still taking down notes. It was a quiet ride down the elevator and once we were on the first floor, we all went our own way, nothing was said.

Retail has busy months and slow months and when it is slow, wow it is slow. That is what March was like and the only holiday that brought additional shoppers in was St. Patrick's Day. Due to the change in business, some employees left for other jobs where they could make more money and we would hire but management was very sharp and didn't hire excessively. I was tasked to head up a new team with the goal to go out into the community and help in any way that we could. The direction from our store manager, Ashley Kood was simple, make Brissell's a household name and whatever we do, be sure we do it with class. I was rather surprised that she put me in charge and there were others in the store that looked at me having this task as being a bit, no more like a huge contradiction. I heard things that were being said and was surprised when I heard that our head of finance, Bonnie Whyt was laughing at lunch shortly after the announcement was made. The story was that she was talking to Pam Whaz, Rhonda May and others and someone said that they couldn't believe that a man like me and the words I heard were and I quote, 'How could Rob Brewstard be asked to work on something so big when he is always looking out for his own happiness and at the expense of others.' Not sure who said this but I was shocked to even think that this might have been said. I thought this comment had to come from someone other than Bonnie, Pam or Rhonda and my reaction was I would prove to whoever said this about me was wrong. I would put Brissell's in front of me and I would do everything without looking for any kind of reward, my new motto was simple, do for others first.

It was a Wednesday evening and I knew I had to get started on getting my team together but up to this point, I was the team. This was heavy on my mind and I couldn't get to sleep till close to eleven and when I did, I tossed and turned most of the night thinking about what to do. At one point I woke up and looked at the alarm clock and it was three and I had a few choice words that I yelled out. I then hit my pillow repeatedly like a boxer hitting an opponent. After this outburst, I must have finally fallen asleep and woke up at six. My mind at the point was clear; I had an idea and would follow up with it at work right after the morning sales meeting.

One of the first things I needed to do was to bring on board two others and knew I needed to pick the right ones. I did this by walking around all three floors of the store, watching the sales clerks, the cashiers, the floor stockers and I also walked through the offices. I was a little shocked by the administrative offices when I saw Bonnie Whyt, Pam Whaz and Rhonda May; I could see in their faces that deep down they felt that I was not the right person for this new team however, I didn't let anything nor anyone bring me down and warmly wished them a great day and thanked them for all that they do for the store. Crazy, their facial expressions seemed to instantly change and they now had beautiful and happy smiles. My new motto was firmly in my heart and I let my heart do the talking and I could see that my actions and words were affecting others. One thing I needed to do was to be sure that the two individuals I would recruit to be on the team would have the same value as I now had and follow my motto, do for others first.

I spent Thursday looking for the right team members, working till closing and I was at the store a couple of hours before it opened on Friday wanting to see how the departments were restocked and how our great cleaning crew made the store spotless. Friday flew by and over the weekend, I didn't have time to search; I had to watch over the sales associates in my department.

Monday and Tuesday of the next week went by and I finally made my decision late Tuesday; Wendy Wood and Jinny Shapely were going to be my right hand team members and at the last minute I also picked Susan Shapley for the team. I was very happy with my selections and informed them early Wednesday and through quick visits to their work areas and through phone calls we planned to meet on Friday evening at five; this was the best time to get everyone together. This meeting would be a get to know one another and come up with our game plan. To make it informal, we decided to meet at a nearby restaurant; our goal was simple, make this our getting acquainted team meeting and to come up with our goals for helping out our community. I updated our store manager with the news of our upcoming meeting and she was quite pleased to know that things were moving in the right direction for the event.

The rest of the week flew by and we had a reservation at a nearby casual home-style restaurant. I was there early and was seated at a table in the back as I previously had requested. As each of the ladies arrived, I was the perfect gentleman and warmly welcomed them. Things started off rather slowly at dinner, not too much talking but as soon as the dessert hit the table, we all opened up about family, careers, and ourselves. An after dinner drink helped break the ice as well.

Wendy Wood spoke up first, "Hi all and I am Wendy Wood and I work in Womenswere as the Lead Sales Associate; I moved here from New Mexico. My past experience was working at hotels as a Desk Clerk and Customer Service Rep and when I moved here, I made a career change to working in department stores. First, small stores and after five years, I left and moved to Brissell's and worked my way up to my current position and I love it here."

"Wendy, are you married?"

"A bit too personal Rob."

"Sorry Wendy, I'm only asking because I think I worked with you at the Grand View Hotel in Albuquerque; that was a long time ago when I was in my early twenties."

"And Rob didn't you used to have a full head of hair and a curly beard?"

"Sure did and didn't you used to have red hair?"

"Yes, and over the years I took up yoga along with running five miles every weekend. I changed my hair back to my natural color and divorced the man that I thought I would love the rest of my life. My maiden name back then was…"

I smiled and blurted out, "You used to be Wendy Day and I remember that I asked you out on a date; you shot me down faster than, excuse the way this sounds, a speeding bullet."

"That's right Rob, now I remember; you were trying to be a real…"

I quickly moved on, "Well thank you Wendy and let's welcome Jinny Shapley to the team and Jinny, tell us about yourself."

"I am Shapely, not Shapley and you were the one I slapped during the team-bonding meeting we had back at Mindors Department Store in Kansas. Remember that Rob?"

I was stunned, "Are you sure about that Ms. Shapely?"

"Yes Rob and I hope you have grown up and no longer the same man as you used to be. No wise cracks please about my last name; when I married the love of my life, the marriage crumbled after one year and two months."

"I'm sorry to hear that Jinny. One question, your last name is still Shapely, why didn't you keep your last name from the marriage?"

You Must Be Kidding Me

"My husband turned out to be not so nice of a man and I simply wanted to go back to my maiden name after the divorce."

"Sorry to ask, but what was it?"

Jinny hesitated and softly said, "Jestbig."

With a slight chuckle, "Seriously, you were Jinny, Jinny Jestbig?"

"Yes Rob, I knew you would make fun of it but like your last name, the T is silent."

"I can see why you went from Jestbig back to Shapely. "

"Anyway, I am like Wendy, a Lead Sales Associate and I also do all of the store's videos for self improvement."

"And Jinny what is your main department?"

"Oh, I forgot to tell you, I work in Women's Lingerie."

I started to reply but before I said something that I would regret, Susan broke into the conversation, "Please don't confuse me and Jinny Shapely, I am Shapley, Susan Shapley and Rob... you had better remember when I turned twenty-one and the night we had at the hotel in San Antonio, remember that?"

You Must Be Kidding Me

I turned red, "That was you Susanne?"

With a raised voice, "Not Susanne it is Susan and Rob did you forget about the dinner and dancing?"

"That was it?"

"Yes Rob, nothing else happened but what happened with Susanne?"

I quickly changed the topic "And Susan, please tell the other ladies what department you are in."

Susan's voice changed to that of a professional speaker, "Part of the time I do our overhead voice announcements and the rest of the time, my main job is Inventory Control; if something is on the shelves here at Brissell's, I had my hands on getting it there"

"Regarding your voice gig, what exactly does that cover Susan?"

"I do all the voices you hear throughout the store for our sales promotions."

"It was a no brainer why I picked you, I heard your voice and it was full of passion."

"I am touched by that Rob and speaking of passion…"

You Must Be Kidding Me

Before Susan could say anything else I took over the conversation, "So team, we are going to make Brissell's a household name and we will be doing this by being the department store that does for others before we think of ourselves. In other words, we are doing for others first. Let's talk about what we can do, Jinny please go first."

She didn't hesitate to reply, "How about we form a team of those who work here who have construction experience? We can use them to help some homeowners within let's say a two-mile radius around the store with a special room remodel, maybe like new kitchen cabinets or painting a room or two in their house. Not too sure how to pull this off but this would be a great way to show that we care."

"Alright, and thank you Jinny." Susan, what idea do you have?"

"I think we should do something here at the store for all of our customers; what about we give out coupons over the next week for discounts. We can have discounts of ten, twenty, and thirty percent and then on one day, early morning we could open the store but only for those who have the discount coupons and we can have free coffee, juice, and pastries for all. I think this would be a great way to show that we care."

You Must Be Kidding Me

"Good going Susan and Wendy, what do you have?"

"Why not do something real simple like a carwash; I know this might sound rather lame but we can do free car washes for the next two weeks over the weekend and it would be for anyone, not just those who have recently shopped here. That would be a real we care for our community and not just those who shop here. If this idea flies, I can talk to the manager of the gas station on the corner of the mall and see if we can use their location."

"Like that idea Wendy. So ladies, I will take your ideas to Ashley Kood and let her pick one. Does that sound reasonable? Jinny, what do you think?

"Way to go Rob, good going."

Susan added, "I am sure that whichever idea Ashley picks will be great and well supported by the four of us and the whole store."

"And Wendy, do you agree?"

"Yes indeed and I am pleased to be working with you along with Jinny and Susan on this wonderful caring event for our community."

I paused after the three ladies spoke and then it came to me, "Each of you had such wonderful ideas and you used similar words including care and it just came to me, how about if we call the event, 'We Care for You.' What do you think?"

The three ladies all agreed and it was up to me to present this the next day to management. With that out of the way, we had another after dinner drink and toasted to what would be a special event for Brissell's.

The next day I went straight to the admin offices to meet with Ashley to update her on the first meeting I had last with the three ladies. She was a bit busy and after waiting about ten minutes, she opened her office door and I followed her in.

"Good morning Rob, how are you this morning?"

"Well I couldn't be any better, and you Ashley?"

"I am fine, just fine. Please have a seat Rob."

She directed me to the oversized leather chairs located to the side of her office; after we were seated she reached for a pen and writing pad and continued, "I hear happiness in your voice; guess that has something to do with your dinner meeting last night?"

"Yes I am happy and yes it's due to the meeting with the team members I picked for the event."

You Must Be Kidding Me

"Tell me Rob, who did you choose to work with and why?"

"I knew from the start that I needed individuals that would work hard and most important, those who are proud to represent our store to the local community."

"Sounds like you are starting off on the right foot Rob, please continue."

"Wendy Wood and Jinny Shapely, both Sales Associates and Susan Shapley from Inventory Control and she also does our overhead promotions."

"I know all three and you picked three winners; please elaborate on each one."

"Wendy Wood was a perfect choice."

"Why Ms. Wood?"

"I watched her on the floor and could tell that she would be a great representative for what our store stands for and what we want to do for our event."

"That's it Rob? You just knew Wendy Wood would deliver that special quality that we have here at Brissell's?"

You Must Be Kidding Me

"Yes, I felt that from the first time I saw her working, such a great attitude toward the customers and she was always smiling. When she spoke, her voice was quite pleasant."

"Sounds good and what about Jinny Shapely, what was it about her and why did you want her on your team?"

"She had that special look of caring and when talking to her customers, her voice was very sincere. I also saw that her customers felt comfortable talking to her. I knew that Jinny would be wonderful for the team."

Ms. Kood continued, "What about Susan Shapley?"

"I picked her for the team when I happened to be in Bonnie Whyt's office and she was in the adjacent room doing a promo for the store. I heard something in her voice, a caring; a passion for Brissell's and knew that she would be a great addition to the team."

"Sounds like you were very thorough Rob picking your team and I'm pleased with your choices."

"Thank you Ashley."

"Now then Rob, what are the actual ideas you have for the event?

You Must Be Kidding Me

"Each of the ladies had great ideas and each was so different. One was to have free car washes for anyone and it could be at the corner gas station here at the mall. Another was to do home remodeling for homeowners who live near the store, and the third was to give out discounts for our customers to use here and at a special time. I like all three and have combined them into a one-day event here at the store and it would begin two hours before our normal opening time. We would have discount cards that could be given out as customers enter and they could be used when returning on a different day. We would also do the carwash starting at this same time and it would extend till mid afternoon and regarding the home remodeling, I would like your opinion and see what you come up with. And by the way, based off of what each lady said, we came up the name for the event and it is so perfect!"

"What is it Rob?"

"Our event name is, 'We Care for You.' "

Ashley didn't say a thing and I saw that she was in deep thought. About a full minute passed, "First of all Rob, you did a great job picking your team and they came up with great ideas for our event and I love the name. You are putting it together in a wonderful way and I'm pleased that you are the team lead. Now, regarding the home remodel, how about we simply have the same discount cards but with ten having something on them, like a gold star, which would be for the lucky customers receiving the room makeovers. The makeovers would allow them to pick from our different departments such as Furniture, Drapes, Bedspreads, and things like that. What do you think?"

"That is perfect and I can see this as the ultimate way Brissell's cares for our customers."

With that the meeting ended and I went back to work and as the day went on, I went to the departments where Wendy, Jinny and Susan worked and gave them the news on the event. Needless to say, the three were ecstatic and we were ready to do whatever was needed to make the event a total success.

The days and weeks flew by as we all did different things to plan, publicize and meet with other departments. We all did just about anything and everything we could think of to get to our final goal, the event itself that would be held on the upcoming Sunday morning. One thing for sure, the three ladies and I were confident it would be a total success. One cool thing we added just days before the event and that was a tent and it would be placed in the parking lot and used for the central gathering point.

Sunday arrived and the team was there early to set up the tent and coordinate the day's activities. We worked so hard to get the tent ready and like the store; it opened two hours prior to the normal opening time. In the tent, we had lots of pastries including donuts and danish, bagels with cream cheese, toast and jellies and three types of coffee and four different varieties of juices. To make it easier for our guests, we had four of these locations set up within the tent. In addition to giving out discounts to our store, we had monetary gift cards that our guests could use at any store and just not ours. This was important and our upper management came up with this as the ultimate gesture showing that we do care for our current customers and new friends. Jinny, Susan, Wendy and myself were totally happy and so were all the managers and directors in attendance; we really pulled it off!

There was one other thing that happened and I was rather surprised by it. I was there about an hour before the tent opened and as I walked around checking on things, I ran into one person whom I hardly expected to see.

"Well, good morning Rob, how are you?'

I knew that voice and turned around, "Detective Lockheart, good morning to you and I am perfectly fine this morning; how are you?"

"Doing well; do you have a minute to spare?"

You Must Be Kidding Me

I looked at my watch and then back to Lenah, "I'm a bit busy right now getting ready for the start of our event."

"Please Rob, call me Lenah and is it alright if I walk around with you for a bit?"

I knew I really didn't have a choice, "Sure Lenah, I am going to check on the continental breakfast stations we are providing for our guests; I'm sure they are ready if you want something to eat to start your day?"

"That's great and I could use something to get me going; it looks like I will have a busy day."

I was puzzled, "You mean here as in here in the tent?"

"Yes and also around the carwash and walking the floors of the store."

Still puzzled, "And how did this come about Lenah?"

"It was a few days ago, Emery Knot called me and asked that I be here, just checking out the event."

I walked Lenah over to the tables where the goodies were already set up, "Well this is indeed a surprise having you here and I feel safer already.

You Must Be Kidding Me

Please enjoy and I have to run off and check the other food areas and on…"

Lenah interrupted me, "Please go ahead, I will do what Knot asked me to do and I am sure I will see you at some point throughout the rest of the day."

With that, I was off; still puzzled why Emery asked her to be here but he must have had his reasons.

The day zipped by like a bullet train in Japan and before we knew it, the 'We Care for You' event was over and everyone enjoyed his or her day with us at Brissell's. The tent was a huge success and our customers took advantage of the discounts to shop till they dropped and the carwash was a success beyond words; it was helped by the perfect weather. Ten extremely happy families were the recipients of the special discount cards with the gold stars. All in all, a perfect day and at the end of the day, I ran into Lenah and she had a good time at our event. We didn't talk other than her telling me this and saying goodbye.

The event was a total success due to the driving force of the three outstanding women, Wendy Wood, Jinny Shapely and Susan Shapley. All of our departments were involved in one or more phases of the event and this included everything from the planning to promotion, from the decorating to cleanup, from the special guests that were invited and to those who will write the thank you letters of appreciation that will be sent later in the week. I was so thankful to all departments and I would not have been able to pull off the event if not for the three ladies who went beyond what I had even dreamt of when Ms. Kood asked me to be the lead to the event. Our management was so wonderful and they showed how much they care for us, the employees.

What did this do for our store? Well, we showed that we care for our customers and hopefully new friends of Brissell's. From the very beginning, Ms. Kood told me and I followed up by telling Wendy, Jinny and Susan that we were doing this to show our caring for our customers and at no time wore we to think about the end result and to our profit margin. We showed our customers and new friends and the merchants around our store how much we care for them. To sum it up, we were all winners.

It was late Tuesday afternoon following the event that Ms. Kood called me to her office and to my surprise, Emery Knot and Bonnie Whyt were there and there was one more person in attendance however, I didn't know who she was.

Ashley started the meeting, "Rob, I am glad that you are here and thank you so much for your great planning and direction for the 'We Care for You' event."

You Must Be Kidding Me

"I was so pleased to be a part of it, I love Brissell's and I put everything I had into the event; you were the one who picked me and thank you so much for giving me the opportunity. You gave me confidence and I know this is what I conveyed to my wonderful team."

Ashley went on to say, "Rob, I would like you to meet our regional VP over Sales and Marketing, Theresa Day."

I reached out toward her and she extended her hand and a nice handshake ensued, "I am pleased to meet you Rob and have some great news for you."

Our handshake ended, "So nice to meet you Ms. Day."

She continued, "For your effort, and I mean you, Wendy, Jinny and Susan, we will rent out the largest ballroom we can find at one of the local hotels for a party for all of our employees. Everything from appetizers to dinner and dessert and drinks will be offered to all at no cost. It is the way the entire region's administrative staff wants to show how much we care and this is our way of giving back to you."

I was really shocked by her generosity, "This is amazing and I can't believe you are doing this!"

You Must Be Kidding Me

"This is the least that we can do for our amazing employees."

By chance Ms. May, do you have a date for the party?"

"Not yet Rob, but it will be up to Ms. Kood to finalize the date but we would like to have it as soon as possible and April first seems to be the best date. What do you think?"

Hearing this, my first thought was rather skeptical, "I appreciate the party Ms. Day but on April Fools' Day?"

Ashley interjected, "This does seem to be the best date for the party; first of the month and the beginning of spring."

Ms. Day followed, "I agree with Ashley, April first is the best date and I say we move on to book it."

I was outnumbered and knew it would be best to continue to be a team member, "Then the date is fine for me; I am thankful that you are doing this for our employees."

Theresa added, "On behalf of me, Ms. Kood, Ms. Whyt, and Mr. Knot, thank you Rob for everything you did for the 'We Care for You' event and we do care for you."

You Must Be Kidding Me

I was touched by her words and went up to everyone in the room and shook hands with them. I couldn't leave the room without having the last words, "Thank you all and a pleasant evening to you."

With that, I left and went straight to my car; as I drove home I reflected upon the meeting. It was great being recognized for what I did for the event but when I think about it, picking the wonderful three ladies was the key to the success; I was a small cog in the big wheel. It was great that the upper leaders of Brissell's decided to have a party to acknowledge everyone because we all and I mean all of us worked toward showing how we do care for the community. This goes for not only those who were in front of the scenes, you know like cashiers, sales clerks, and so many others but if not for the efforts of those who work behind the scenes such as the janitorial staff, maintenance, stockers and so many others, well without everyone the event would not have been such a resounding success.

As I hit the pillow, I was wide-awake and still thinking about the party to be held on the first of April. I was pleased that having the date set for the party was good but now the hard part would be who Ms. Kood would pick to head it up. I had my own feelings as to whom it should be but decided not to talk to her about it however, a part of me, actually a huge part of me wanted to be on the committee. I quickly squashed this thought and cleared it from my mind. The only remaining thought I had had to do with working on Monday as well as today; my time in the department was a bit off. I could tell I was out of my work rhythm but after another day or two working would surely fix that. The last thing I did was to turn off the light next to my bed.

The next morning I met with Ms. Kood and she informed me that Wendy Wood would be over the April Fools' Day party and that Emery Knot and not I would assist. I took the news in stride and was pleased by her choices; I had total confidence that Wendy Wood would be fine and Emery Knot was a good choice as well. As always, Ashley did a great job placing employees in different departments together to come together as one. With this news, I felt that the spring party would be another Brissell's success. Other than the party being on April Fools' Day, I was totally looking forward to it.

It was the next day, I was shocked when I received a call from Emery with news that Wendy, Jinny and Susan didn't show up for work on Monday and he asked me to contact each of their managers and see what information they might have. I was requested to contact their families in person; I had become good friends with each during the 'We Care for You' event. The conversation with Emery was very short and very direct.

You Must Be Kidding Me

After the call, I immediately phoned Ashley, "I just received notice from Emery and he filled me in on the situation with Jinny, Wendy and Susan and I am dumbfounded. I will make the calls to their managers and families."

Ashley replied, "Thank you so much Rob, I know how much the ladies mean to you and I feel pain in your words. Please go in person to meet with the families, it will be the best thing to do."

"Thank you and after our morning sales team meeting, I will start my calls and arrange family visits."

The sales meeting was much shorter than the normal time, only fifteen minutes; once it finished, I was off to my office to make calls to the different managers. Each call resulted in the same thing, no one had any news about the ladies other than what we knew and that was that they didn't show up for work.

I then called each of the families and they had the same story and that was that ladies left for work at the same time they always did and nothing seemed unusual. I asked if I could come by and meet with them but each family rejected my request. I checked back with the department managers and they didn't have anything new to report. I was not sure what else I could do other than asking for help from Emery and yes, I knew we would have to call

You Must Be Kidding Me

Detective Lockheart and let her know that once again we had employees that are missing.

It was later that day that Emery called me to his office to meet with him and Lenah and when I opened the door, they greeted me. After our pleasantries, you know shaking hands, how you are and things like that, Lenah spoke first.

"Emery called me this morning with information that three ladies didn't show up for work and their department managers have no information on this. Correct Rob?"

I nodded yes.

"And is this not the third time this kind of thing has occurred?"

Emery jumped in, "Yes Detective, it is."

"No Knot, not you I was asking Rob."

I spoke up with a sigh, "Yes Lenah this is the third time employees have failed to show up to work and yet again, they have seemed to have disappeared. I don't have any information to share other than what I am sure Knot has already filled you in, right Emery?"

Emery replied, "Yes, I know nothing other than what the managers have told me and what Rob has found out after talking to the families of the missing ladies."

"Alright, let's go over the facts starting with who is missing and then we will talk about the event held over the weekend, alright? Please start Rob."

"I picked the three ladies to be part of the event and I worked with them pretty much each day from the time we put the team together to the time of the event."

"What are their names?"

"Jinny Shapely, Susan Shapley and Wendy Wood."

"Okay Rob, so we have Shapely and Shapley and once again, who was the third?"

"That would be Wendy Wood, Lenah."

"I got it; we have Jinny Shapley and Susan Shapely."

I corrected Lenah, "No, Jinny is Shapely and Susan is Shapley."

"Sorry 'bout that Rob."

"And don't forget Lenah, the third was Wendy Wood."

You Must Be Kidding Me

"I have her down on my notes."

"Alright Lenah, what else do you want to know?"

"So you picked them by yourself without any help from anyone else, is that right Rob?"

"That is correct. I found them to be the best fit for the team and happy that they accepted to be part of it."

"Did you work well with them and did they work well with you?"

"We would."

"Is that just Wendy?"

"Just Wendy what Lenah?"

"I am asking if it was just Wendy Wood that you worked well with."

"Not at all Lenah, I also worked well with Susan and Jinny."

"Was this the first time you worked with her?"

"With which one?"

"Wendy."

"Actually Lenah, I worked with her in Albuquerque."

"And what about Jinny and Susan?"

"What about them Lenah?"

"Did you know them prior to Brissell's and if so where?

"Only Susan, I worked with her in San Antonio."

"Just curious Rob, did you pick these two ladies because you worked with them in the past?"

"Actually Lenah, it was a while back and I didn't even recognize them when I was searching for the employees to be on the team."

"Rather interesting Rob, can you explain?"

"It wasn't till the four of us got together for dinner when we did introductions that they brought up our past working relationships."

"So you had a relationship with each of the ladies?"

"Only Wendy and Susan."

You Must Be Kidding Me

"So you are saying you had a relationship with Wendy and Susan, is that correct?"

I was taken by her question, "Only a work relationship Lenah, nothing more."

"Alright, I have that noted and now what about during the event; did you and the ladies have any arguments?"

I paused, as I didn't like her question or her tone, "Detective, are you thinking that I had something to do with their disappearance?"

Emery quickly jumped in, "No Rob, I don't think she is insinuating any such thing is that right Lenah?"

"No Knot, not at all, just getting information for my notes. So Rob was everything fine with you and the ladies during the event?"

With a bit of a harsh tone I replied, "We had a great working relationship from our first meeting all the way through the conclusion of the event. When everyone had left the party, the four of us helped with cleaning and some of the tear down and then we all said goodnight to one another and went our separate ways."

"So everything was fine?"

You Must Be Kidding Me

With a raised and sharp voice, "Yes, everything was fine Lenah."

"Did you see anything unusual Knot?"

"No, nothing at all."

Lenah continued, "Not a thing at all Knot?"

Emery shook his head as if to say no.
Lenah stood up from the chair she was sitting on and replied, "Thank you Emery and Bob, if you can think of anything, anything at all please call me and once again, I will keep you and Knot informed with any new news I have."

"Knot replied, "Thank you Lenah and Rob, I appreciate you coming up to speak to the detective."

I replied, "Lenah, you just called me Bob."

"I know that, just wanting to have fun with you."

So that was it, I went back to work and looked forward to the rest of the week.

Here at Brissell's, we can make a party out of just about anything. I was not going to volunteer to do anything for any other parties and knew darn well that I would not be asked. I guess that I have some odd karma when it comes to parties or events; seems they are always marked by wonderful ladies working for us disappearing. I am guessing this is why our store manager passed on me for being part of the April Fools' Day party. The dilemma now would be whom would she pick if Wendy Wood was not available? I quickly realized what I was thinking and then said to myself that there was a logical reason why the three of them didn't show up for work.

A couple of days went by and there was no good or bad news regarding the ladies and nothing at all from Lenah. I was surprised that I didn't hear anything at all but that actually in an interesting way turned out to be a good thing. I was not going to be doing anything for the April Fools' Day party and that was perfect, I had been seeing Tiffany, a delightful young lady for the past two months who was eight years younger than me. Pretty cool, a gorgeous twenty-seven year old woman with so many men that would love the chance to be with her and she was with me. I must say that since we started dating and when she would come by the store and we had lunch at one of the many restaurants in the mall, I could feel other men staring at us; for that matter, women too were checking us out. I felt that the guys were envious, after all, look at the gorgeous woman I was with. My strange thinking process had me to believe that the women scoping us out were wishing that they were with me, like I said, strange thinking on my part.

You Must Be Kidding Me

I was indeed the lucky one and Tiffany was by far the most amazing woman I had ever dated and our relationship started on that wonderful New Year's Eve party. It was such a fluke thing that happened I was getting a glass of champagne and as I was walking toward the front of the room, a clumsy guy bumped into the woman who was walking next to me and she slipped and ran into me. I wound up falling to the ground and then as I was getting up, I grabbed hold of a chair and pulled myself to a somewhat vertical position. This gal who bumped into me then made a fist and turned around to clobber the clumsy guy but he ducked and she connected with my chin and knocked me out cold. I was down for the count and remember looking up and thinking that I was dreaming as this goddess was looking at me; her hand was intertwined with my right hand. She helped me partially up but I was still lying somewhat on the ground. I didn't budge for what seemed the longest minute or two in my life and then this unknown woman helped me up to a chair. So, that was our first meeting and after that evening, actually morning I did not see her and had no knowledge who she was. I felt like what a way to start the New Year and had only a bruised chin and ego to show from this fluke encounter.

So most of January flew by and then one day, the woman who accidentally hit me on New Year's Eve reappeared. I was working and she walked into Menswear; I was mesmerized by her and I can still picture that day in my mind as clear as clear can be.

You Must Be Kidding Me

She was not too short and not too tall, I guess she was just the perfect height. Her long light brunette hair was straight and she wore a tan long sleeved blouse with a blue skirt that stopped a few inches above her knees. She had on black heels and a smile that would light up a totally dark room. I was dumbfounded and then when she saw me, she walked over and we actually talked and I was in like at first sight, well second sight. Perfect timing as it was my break and we left the store and walked over to a bench outside of a jewelry store. Strange thought filled my mind, I remember a dream I had that I was buying a diamond engagement ring at this store but that was it, no idea who it was for. Now, I found a diamond and a priceless one at that.

The rest of March went by rather quickly and as I was previously saying, I was glad that I didn't have the responsibility of doing anything for the upcoming April Fools' Day party. My life now was concentrating on two things, Tiffany and my career; the party was going to happen no matter what, even if I had no part in it. I was curious though if anything happened with Windy, Jinny and Susan and on Friday, one day prior to the party, I went to Ashley's office and asked if there was any news.

"Actually Rob, we had a follow up call from Detective Lockheart earlier today and she told me that the ladies still have not been seen at home and it is like they just vanished."

You Must Be Kidding Me

"That is so odd Ashley; I hope that Detective Lockhart has some good news for us soon."

"I hope so all well, anything else I can help you with?"

I hesitated, "Just curious, not that I need to know, but who is working with Emery on the party?"

"Well Rob, Emery was so busy with the investigation regarding the three ladies so he politely pulled himself off the planning committee and I have two wonderful young ladies who will be heading up the planning and the party itself."

"Do I know them?"

"I think you do Rob, Terri Toobee and Shandra Lance. Terri works in our collection department and has been with us for five years. Shandra was a Lead Sales Associate for eight years at one of our sister stores and moved here a little over a year ago. Both are doing great and I am thrilled to have them on board for the party."

"Sounds like a great duo, I am sure they will put on a great party."

"Thank you Rob for stopping in and I heard that you have a girlfriend."

You Must Be Kidding Me

"I do and surprised that you know about it; her name is Tiffany and as strange as it sounds, I love her and I think she loves me."

"You don't know Rob?"

"No, I haven't said the L word to her, nor has she said it to me. I am using the April Fools' Day party as the time to tell her how I feel."

Ashley smiled, "Well best fortune to you and Tiffany."

"Thank you for your kind words Ashley."

With that I left and finished a few things at my desk and then I was off to meet Tiffany for dinner. I first stopped at a store right around the corner from Brissell's and purchased a gift for her and then walked down the mall to the restaurant. The minute I walked into the restaurant, I saw her and she looked breathtaking. I walked up to her, we kissed and I gave her the single red rose that I had just stopped for.

We had a delightful dinner and we walked to her car and we shared a nice hug and kiss; she left for home. I walked back toward Brissell's and then to the parking garage and to my car; the whole drive home I wondered why I didn't tell Tiffany at dinner or when kissing her goodbye what I really wanted to say. I knew that I would find the right time and it would be rather special.

Later that evening I called her and we talked for over an hour. We set the time that I would pick her up for the party and I so wanted to say something more to her other than good night my dear. I was holding back on saying what I really wanted to say till the party; I decided this would be the best time to tell her that I was in love with her.

Saturday was downright torturous; it went by so slowly. I had planned this day to do spring cleaning in the garage but other than this, nothing to do till the time I needed to get ready for the party. Throughout the day I found myself drawn to the phone and talking to Tiffany which I did twice and she called me once. I was in love and was so anxious to finally tell her but for now; the L word would have to wait till later that evening.

It was four when I stopped cleaning and took a shower, put on my tux as I did for all of our parties and went to pick up Tiffany. She lived only ten minutes away and my heart was all but ready to jump out from within my chest, as I was so nervous for this night to happen and telling her my true feelings. I kept taking deep breaths the whole drive and when I arrived at her house, I had calmed down. I parked, checked myself out in the rear-view mirror and opened the car door. It would have helped if I had unbuckled the seat belt but only a minor dumb thing on my part; I blew it off due to being in love.

I walked up the brick sidewalk and rang the bell; she appeared like an angel from heaven and it seemed like she floated out of her house as she closed the door. Being the gentleman that I am; I escorted her down the brick walkway and opened the car door for her. After she was in, I walked to my door, got into the car and looked her way, "You are incredible and mere words cannot express how I feel about you and how beautiful you look tonight."

Tiffany followed that by saying, "You look pretty sharp as well, and you clean up nicely."

The drive to the hotel was only five minutes and as I pulled up, the valet attendant was there to take the car. I gave him the keys and opened the door for Tiffany and we went up the elevator to the party. The next three hours were at times funny as April Fools' Day jokes were played on Ashley, Emery, and other managers. Between the joking, dinner was great and the dancing afterwards was the best ever; after all, I had the most wonderful woman in my arms and I was just getting ready to kiss her when the announcement was made, "The pool on the roof will be open for the next hour and anyone who would like to partake in a late night swim under the full moon, please jump on in. We have lots and lots of swimsuits available for you straight from our stores and they will be available for our customers by the first of May."

Well, who could resist this; Tiffany and I joined others in the nearby elevator and were off to the roof. Once there, I went to the men's changing room and Tiffany left for the women's changing room. About five minutes passed and I was patiently waiting for Tiffany to emerge and when she did, she was wearing a one-piece black swimsuit that fit her like a glove. I walked to her, took her hand and placed it to my heart; I took a breath and said, "You have entered my heart in a way that no one else has and..."

I was stopped right there as a co-worker yelled out to us, "Come on you two lovebirds, let's go swimming!"

Tiffany and I casually walked over to the pool and stood at the edge; other employees were already swimming or ready to jump in. Pam Whaz was already in and said, "Come on in you two, the water is perfect."

"Isn't it cold?"

"Only for a minute Rob, then you will be fine."

I looked over to Tiffany and she was looking deep into my eyes and as she was beginning to say something, a hand was on my back and I was pushed into the pool. A second or two later, Tiffany was in the pool as well and yes the water was cold but we quickly adjusted to it. This was such a memorable time and we swam under the full moon with about thirty of our co-workers and their spouses or significant others. The outdoor lights were off and the lights within the pool were off as well; the moonlight was all that was needed and it was so romantic.

Everyone was having a great time; Tiffany and I were not really swimming, we were more like dancing together, holding each other so closely. I felt that I was about ready to tell her what I so wanted to but then, a woman's voice filled the air.

"This is Detective Lockheart from the police department; we have to ask you all to leave the pool. Please go to the dressing rooms and change and leave the building at once."

At that same time, the lights around the pool came on and the enjoyment turned to uncertainty. As I helped my dear Tiffany from the pool we walked over to Lenah.

"Good evening Lenah, what is going on?"

"Gee Rob, go figure, you are right here when yet another missing person has been reported."

You Must Be Kidding Me

I was stunned, "Come on Lenah, this is not a nice April Fools' Day joke to play on me."

Tiffany looked at me and said, "Do you know this woman?"

"Yes dear, through work."

"Is that all or do I need to know more about her?"

"No Tiffany, work only."

Lenah interrupted, "Why don't you two change and as I requested, leave the building. I will see you tomorrow Rob when I visit your management; I bet that they can hardly wait to see me. Mark it on your calendar, meeting at one."

Lenah chuckled and Tiffany and I left for the dressing rooms and once we changed, we immediately left the building as requested. We had to wait about ten minutes to get the car and we really didn't talk much on the way back to her house however, once we arrived, I opened the car door and walked her to the front door; we kissed and then I said what I was waiting to say all evening, "I love you Tiffany."

We kissed again and then she said, "Good night my shining knight, I love you too."

You Must Be Kidding Me

With that, April Fools' Day was over. I drove off with the love of my life deeply entrenched in my heart and mind. I was so happy and that happiness was with me through my drive home and throughout the night. I slept like a baby and when the alarm went off at five, I did my usual routine of exercising, eating breakfast and something new to add to my routine, calling Tiffany to say good morning and love you.

We spoke for only a few minutes; she wished me a good day and called me the love of her life. I was so ready to have a great day; nothing would bring me down, not even visiting with Lenah regarding yet another missing person. I finished getting ready and left for work at seven with love in my heart. Unfortunately I had lots of wonderment running around my head about yet another visit with Detective Lockhart.

I arrived at the mall and pulled into the parking structure and was walking to the store when I heard that all too familiar voice, "Morning, Rob."

I turned around and approaching me on the side was Detective Lockheart, "Good morning Lenah, how are you this fine spring day."

Lenah snickered, "Doing' fine Rob, how are you?"

You Must Be Kidding Me

"Couldn't be better, I am on the top of the world."

"Sounds great, once you get settled can you join me in a meeting with some of your top executives?"

"I already have it marked on my calendar for one. This morning at eight I meet with the other Sales Managers and plan our day. At nine I will be meeting with the sales associates in my department. I am so busy after checking out the floor and then there is lunch; I will be upstairs by one."

"Alright Rob and…"

I was already walking away from her when she spoke out, "Please bring any information you have on Shanda Sed So and Barney to the meeting."

I stopped, turned around and walked back to her, "I barely heard what you were asking. Did you say something about information?"

"Yes, I said bring any information you have on Shanda Sed So and Barney as well."

"Got it, you need information on Shanda and Barney Aswyl."

"Yes Rob, information on both of them."

You Must Be Kidding Me

"Can you be a bit more explicit Lenah on what information you need?"

Lenah replied, "Employee files on Shanda and Barney from Marketing."

I was not too sure which Barney, "Do you want files on Barney in Phone Sales."

"That's right Rob, why is this so hard for you to understand?"

I sure didn't care for her attitude, "So you are referring to Barney Nu, not Barney Aswyl; why didn't you say so?"

Lenah seemed a bit edgy, "I did and don't forget that I also said Sed So."

"I get it; you said that I need to bring information to the meeting on Barney Nu."

"I did, and along with information on Barney, don't forget I said Sed So."

"Still not getting you Lenah, you said so, but said so what?"

"Sorry, that is Shanda Sed So. I also need any information you have on her and Barney Nu."

You Must Be Kidding Me

"Got it Lenah, why didn't you say so from the start."

"I did and maybe Rob, start by getting coffee."

"Alright, I will ask her to pull any files on Barney Nu and Shanda Sed So."

"Who will pull the information?"

"Like you said, Koffee."

"What does coffee have to do with pulling the files on Shanda and Barney?"

"You asked me to bring her."

"Who Rob?"

"Koffee, Sheila Koffee my Admin Assistant who will pull info on both, isn't that what you said you wanted?"

Lenah put a hand to her hip and gave me a look like she wanted to pull my eyes out of their sockets, "Please, just bring whatever information you have on Barney Nu and Shanda Sed So to the meeting at one."

"I will, why didn't you say so." With that I turned around and briskly walked off, I was now running late.

You Must Be Kidding Me

The first meeting lasted the full hour and then the meeting with my team was rather short; I covered all the items I needed to, including the store sales that were coming up. I was so ready to get to work and the minute it finished, I hit the floor and checked out my department and talked to some of our early morning shoppers. It was a bit of a quiet start to the shopping day and I felt comfortable going to my office and getting the information that Lenah requested; I had time as it was only eleven and the meeting was scheduled at one.

When I entered my office, Sheila was on the phone and she pointed to my desk. I walked over and sat down only to see the morning newspaper with a picture on the front page of the swimming pool where we partied last night. Under the picture, the headline read, 'Brissell's employee missing after company party.'

I was shocked seeing this and the short text below read, 'The family of the missing man, wonderful father and husband, called authorities when he failed to come home after a brief stay at a company party that followed dinner at a local hotel. Police checked this out and his car was at the hotel and further investigation found his cell phone by the pool. The family was told by the police that they could not place a missing person's report for 24 hours. The police were given enough information by the family to make them satisfied that indeed he was missing and the report was taken.'

You Must Be Kidding Me

This whole thing was so bizarre and now I knew why Detective Lockhart closed down the party. The man's name was not in the paper however; I put two and two together and knew it was Barney Nu. I was so shocked and sat at my desk wondering what on earth happened to him; just then my desk phone rang and I jumped right out of my chair.

Sheila saw me jump and immediately hung up on her phone call, "Rob, are you alright?"

I was but felt rather embarrassed by the way I jumped from the ringing of the phone, "Thank you for asking, I am just a bit anxious, maybe too much coffee this morning."

"Well, you really seemed bothered by the news about the missing man, any idea who it might be?"

"I have an idea and it came from a detective that was at the party last night and what she said to me when I arrived at work this morning. I think the missing man is Barney Nu."

Sheila took a seat next to my desk, "Did you know Barney Nu?"

"Yes but let's just keep this under wraps for now Sheila; I will find out more information at one when I meet with the detective and management."

"Please let me know if I can help you, alright?"

You Must Be Kidding Me

"Actually Sheila, I was asked by this detective to bring to the meeting any files we have on Barney Nu as well as another employee, Shanda Sed So."

"Sure Rob, I'll look in the file cabinet, do you know where this would be filed?"

"Look in the middle drawer and for the folder marked, promotions."

"I'll find the info for Nu and So in the same folder?"

"Yes Sheila, but it is Sed So."

Sheila had an odd look and replied, "Isn't that what I said?"

"No, you said So but it is Sed So."

Sheila threw her arms up in the air and went over to the file cabinet and within a couple of minutes and with an ecstatic and shrill voice said, "Found it!"

She brought me the folder and I opened it and upon going over my notes, I remembered what happened last year to Barney and for that matter, why Shanda requested a transfer from Family Living to my department. I quickly placed my notes back in the folder and tucked it under my arm and left my office.

You Must Be Kidding Me

"You look a bit flushed Rob, everything alright?"

"Like I said Sheila, too much coffee this morning."

"Shall I get you something before you head to your meeting?"

"No thank you and I appreciate you finding the folder on Barney and Shanda."

"Glad I could help; shall I do anything else for you?"

"No Sheila, if I am not back by three, feel free to leave for the day, after all, you have extra hours accrued helping out on the new spring department updates."

"Well thank you, but what if I get a call from our timekeeper that I clocked out early, should I tell her the reason?"

"Don't worry; just let her know that I said so."

I was almost out of the office when Ashley called me, "Please have your Admin Assistant join us for the meeting, she might be of assistance."

"Alright, we are on our way."

You Must Be Kidding Me

I told Sheila that she was going to join me and she seemed surprised by it. "I will follow you up in just a couple of minutes; I have to finish this letter."

"Okay Sheila, I will save you a seat next to me."

With that, I left and went to the elevator and just my luck; Lenah came from around the corner. We waited and it was only a matter of seconds when the door opened; we walked in and Lenah said, "Good afternoon Rob and how was your morning?"

"I had a good morning; I visited with different managers around the store trying to uncover anything that might help in getting to the bottom of the events from the party."

"I hope to hear about your findings at our meeting."

"I have a lot to share Lenah."

After this exchange of words, both Lenah and I were silent the rest of the ride to the third floor and nothing was said as we exited the elevator and walked into the conference room. I looked around, all the top managers who worked at the store and even others who were at our main office were there. It was weird, all eyes were on me and I had a feeling inside that in addition to questions they had for me about Barney Nu and Shanda Sed So, there would be more information about the other missing employees over the last several months. I took one of the two opened seats at the large oval table and Lenah sat down at another table in the front of the room where Ashley Kood and Emery Knot were seated. Sheila walked in and took the seat next to me.

Emery Knot began, "Good afternoon all, I know everyone is busy with their individual jobs and it is difficult to take time away for a meeting but with that being said, it is important that you are all here. I want to bring everyone up to speed on what happened at the April Fools' Day party beginning with the individuals who were there when it started but were not there, or for that matter anywhere to be found at the end of it."

Ashley then added, "Before you start Emery, I would like to introduce Detective Lenah Lockheart, she has been investigating the other employees who are missing. She has kept me informed every step of the way from our first meeting after the New Year's Eve party and up to where we are today."

"Thank You, I'll do that right now."

Emery then continued, "Thank you Ms. Kood. Detective Lenah Lockheart from police headquarters will conduct the meeting but first for the record, we want everyone here to introduce themselves and their job. Ms. Kood, please begin. After that, we will go around the table from right to left."

You Must Be Kidding Me

"Good afternoon all and thank you for being here. I am Ashley Kood, the Store Manager."

"Emery Knot, head of Security."

"Hello all, I am Rhonda May, the Director of HR."

"And I am Pam Whaz, Rhonda May's Admin Assistant."

"Bonnie Whyt, Corporate Director over Finance."

"Hello everyone, I am the Regional VP over Store Sales and Marketing, Theresa Day."

"Hi there, I am Terri Toobee, most of you know me by my maiden name, Terri Wantz; I worked in China with Crystal."

Lenah, interrupted, "Just to be sure I have this correct, and you worked in the China Department."

"Yes Detective, I worked in China but now I am the Manager of Home Furnishings."

"No longer doing anything with crystal."

"Ashley interjected, "She was referring to Crystal Champion, the first woman who disappeared."

You Must Be Kidding Me

Lenah then said, "Of course, I knew that. Thank you Ms. Wantz, let's continue around the table."

"No, it is Toobee, not Wantz that was my maiden name before I married."

"Anything else to add?"

"Oh yes detective, I worked with Miss Lance on the April Fools' Day party."

"Alright, thank you and next?"

"I am pleased to be here and I am Shandra Lance"

Lenah had a puzzled look on her face, "Who invited you to this meeting Ms. Lance?"

"Please Detective; call me Miss Lance and no it wasn't Whoo."

Lenah nodded and looked through her notepad and then replied, "She was previously married to who?"

Miss Lance replied, "No Detective Lockheart."

Lenah seemed puzzled, "I ask you again Miss Lance, Bonnie Whyt was previously married to who?"

"No not Whoo, it was Walter Woo."

You Must Be Kidding Me

Emery seemed to be dozing off, "Someone called my name?"

"No Emery, I was answering the detectives question and confirming that Bonnie was Woo but married and is now Whyt."

Emery looked a tad bit embarrassed, "Sorry for interrupting, please continue Lenah."

"Thank you Emery. I'm still not sure why Ms. Whyt invited you to the meeting Miss Lance, a lot of items need to be covered in a short period of time and I trust that she had her reason."

Bonnie Whyt glared at Lenah, "Shandra worked with Teri Toobee on the party and I am sure that they will be able to shed light on the issues that we will be discussing if we ever get past the introductions!"

Lenah sensed Bonnie's frustration, "Alright, glad to meet you Miss Lance and look forward to hearing any information you have for us."

"Thank you Lenah, glad to help."

Lenah looked over to the next person, "And who are you"?

You Must Be Kidding Me

"I am Paige Turner and I am here to take notes; our store manager, Ms. Kood asked me if I could be here to document each and every word."

Lenah looked pleased, "Great, I am pleased that someone is here to take notes and Paige, tell me, do you have any legal background?"

Paige smiled brightly, "As a matter of fact, I do Detective Lockheart."

"Well, please fill us in."

Bonnie Whyt interrupted, "A few years ago there was a lawsuit against one of our sister companies and she was so helpful. "

Lenah continued, "She was?"

"Yes, she was. Without Paige, we would not have been able to go over all the legal documents that were presented in court. The documents, excuse me the briefs that we presented were not in an electronic format and we had so many papers in stack after stack and she turned them, one by one. She then gave them to the lawyers as needed."

"Really, she did that Bonnie?"

"Yes Lenah, Paige did that."

You Must Be Kidding Me

Lenah went on to say, "So, Paige Turner was a page turner?"

"I guess you can say that Lenah, but what does that have to do with why we are here? We need to be talking about yet another person who is missing."

"Thank you Bonnie, I am just trying to get a handle on everyone and what their relationship is and was with those who are missing from the first of the year."

"Thank you Lenah, but please let's pick up the speed."

Lenah nodded, "Thank you Paige for being here and next is Mr. Rob Brewstard. For the record, please introduce yourself"

"Lenah, please, remember the "T" is silent."

Lenah smiled and Rob continued, "I am the Sales Director as well as Sales Manager in Menswear and have worked here at Brissell's fourteen years; I love it here and everything we do and stand for. You could even say that I bleed Brissell's Green."

Lenah had a dazed look, "What do you mean by that Rob?"

"Brissell's color scheme is green, a very light green."

You Must Be Kidding Me

"Oh, I get it Rob." Now one question, do you know anything about Barney Nu; his family called Emery Knot last night to report that he never returned from the party. Barney Nu is now officially considered to be missing and a report has been filed regarding his disappearance. Please fill us in on anything you have."

"First of all, I am very sorry to hear this and I pray that Barney will be found and that he is fine."

Ashley added, "Thank you Rob, Barney is such a sweet caring family man. Please continue."

"When I saw you Lenah, earlier this morning you asked me to look for any information on Barney as well as Shanda Sed So; I asked my Admin Assistant, Miss Shelia Koffee to pull the files and I have them."

"Alright Rob, please go ahead and tell us what you have."

I took a deep breath and then a second one, "Barney Nu was the second in command at our On-Line Phone Sales Center and earlier in the year, I passed him up for a promotion by pulling in Shanda Sed So from one of the other stores in Seattle. It was a hard decision picking Shanda over Barney but after her interview, I felt she was the best fit for the job; I was so happy that Ashley flew her in versus doing the interview over the phone. Ashley backed me on this and she even said so in our weekly managers meeting. I was happy that Shanda was going to be with us."

Lenah then questioned me, "How did he take it? Was he really alright with this or did he just suck it up and go with the flow?"

"I felt that he was fine and we talked about it right after the decision and over the next week when Shanda took over her new position. I did what I could to reassure Barney that he was a valuable employee and we at Brissell's were so happy that he was with us."

"And lately Rob, did anything else happen?"

"Well, I spoke to him at the beginning of our party last night and maybe it was the drink or two that he had that brought out a different side of him. I heard in his voice his unhappiness with my decision to promote Shanda Sed So."

"Did he say so?"

"Well, yes. He told me that I could no longer be trusted and that I was not someone who he would consider to be a friend."

"And how did you react?"

You Must Be Kidding Me

"I reiterated to him how much value he brings to the company and how I have so much respect for him as not only an employee but as a man. I felt that my words smoothed over things and that he was cool with the way our talk concluded."

"Thank you for sharing; one last question, did you shake his hand?"

I paused and then replied, "Actually no, I turned around when my beautiful date tapped me on my shoulder."

"So Rob, you left him for your date and that was it?"

"Yes, Lenah. I moved on with her and didn't see Barney the rest of the night."

"Let's switch to Shanda Sed So."

"What do you have to say about her?"

"During the interview process, I talked to Shanda a couple of times over the phone. When we flew her out for an interview, it was the first time we met in person. I was very impressed with everything about her and had a great feeling about what she would bring to Brissell's."

"Are you saying you had feelings for her?"

You Must Be Kidding Me

"Please Lenah, I just met her and my feelings were that she possessed a great personality and everything I asked her, she answered in a way that brought me to the decision right then and there that she would be the best choice for the position."

"Anything else?"

"I saw her again on her first day on the job and early during the April Fools' Day party."

Ashley spoke up, "Please Lenah, what is the reason you are asking so much from Rob, it sounds to me that you are fishing for something that really is not there."

Lenah replied, "I am trying to find out anything that will give me clues as to Barney's disappearance as well as the others who disappeared!"

"Well Lenah, why don't you just ask Rob directly?"

"Alright Ms. Kood. Rob, do you have any idea what might have happened to Barney?"

I looked straight into Lenah's eyes and with a very firm voice replied, "I have no idea what happened to Barney Nu. I am saddened that he has disappeared and as I said during our introductions, I have him and his family in my prayers."

You Must Be Kidding Me

Lenah nodded her head several times and said, "Thank you Rob; no further questions."

Ms. Kood was ready to end the meeting when Lenah asked all in attendance, "Does anyone have anything to add about Barney or Shanda Sed So?"

Terri Toobee quietly spoke up; I have information that might be important about her."

Lenah was just about to stand up but rather quickly took her seat, "Please Ms. Toobee, what do you have?"

"Please call me Terri and I am a good friend with Pam Whaz and saw her with Shanda at the party."

"What did you see Terri."

"Nothing really other than they seemed to be like long time friends."

"In what way?"

"They were sitting at the same table and were talking and laughing a lot. Rhonda May joined them and was laughing along."

"That was it Terri?"

"Yes, Detective and like I said, Pam Whaz was laughing along with Shanda Sed So and Rhonda."

You Must Be Kidding Me

"Well, was there a lot of laughter from all three ladies?"

"I would say Shandra Lance laughed a lot, more than the other two."

Lenah looked exasperated, "Anything else Terri."

"I was in the pool when I saw Pam push Stephanie Wei into the pool."

Lenah was quite inquisitive, "Who is Stephanie Wei."

"She was Pam's roommate not too long ago."

Lenah turned to Pam, "Would you like to say anything about Stephanie Wei."

"Not really, we are very close friends and we have been for over twelve years."

"So why did you push her into the pool? Was it in a malicious way?"

"No way, just having fun with her."

"You mean Stephanie Wei, correct?"

"Yes, that is who you asked me about?"

"Anything else to add about her."

You Must Be Kidding Me

"No Detective, we are like sisters."

Lenah shook her head and then Emery took over the meeting. "I would like to first thank you Detective Lockheart for being here this afternoon and to all who have left your departments, offices or even came in on your time off, thank you so much. Earlier today I spoke with Detective Lockheart and was updated on the other missing employees and there is no new news. I know the families are devastated as we are; Lenah has assured me that the police department is checking every possible lead and leaving no stone unturned."

Emery continued, "Now then, if there are no further questions, I will close the meeting."

Sheila Koffee stood up, "I have a question Mr. Knot."

Knot replied, "Does your question have to with our missing employees?"

"Yes, Mr. Emery, it does."

"That is Knot Miss Koffee."

Sheila had a puzzled look on her face, "Excuse me sir, not what?"

You Must Be Kidding Me

"My last name is Knot; now what do you have to bring to the table Miss Koffee?"

"First, you didn't let me introduce myself to Detective Lockhart."

"I am sorry, please continue."

"I am the Admin Assistant to Mr. Brewstard. I want to say that no one really spoke other than the detective and it seemed that all her questions to Mr. Brewstard were, well I felt accusatory. No questions were asked to anyone else and I have nothing but respect for Mr. Brewstard and enjoy working for him and I support him with all that he does here at the store and admire him greatly."

Emery replied, "Thank you; speaking for everyone, we appreciate your kind words for Rob. If there is nothing else, good afternoon, meeting adjourned."

As all in attendance began to leave the room, it was a moment in my career here at Brissell's that I will not forget. Everyone except for Lenah was showing his or her appreciation toward me, shaking my hand, giving me a high five or a hardy pat on the back. I felt great and now it was just Sheila and me. I reached over to her and we shared a nice boss to Admin Assistant hug. "Thank you so much Sheila for your very kind words."

You Must Be Kidding Me

"I meant every word I said."

With that, the hug ended and we left the room and took the elevator back down to the first floor and went our separate ways. I went to my department and Sheila went to our office. This was quite an interesting day; it started a bit weird but it ended in a wonderful way. The only thing that topped it was my lovely girlfriend called me and told me that we had reservations for dinner at five and to stop by her place and she would be ready for a special night on the town.

The rest of April flew by and it was now May first and for the first time this year, no party at the beginning of the month but that was soon to change. It was at high noon when I received a call from our store manager.

"Good afternoon Ashley, how are you?'

"I'm fine Rob, and I have news about a May party for just our management staff; this includes mid management and up. I have already picked the two employees who are planning the party and the theme is Halloween in May. The date will be on Saturday the fifteen and will be held at a local hotel but we have yet to work out which hotel it will be."

"Interesting time to have a party, we usually have our store parties coinciding with holidays."

You Must Be Kidding Me

"I know, but why not? Oh yes, one other reason for the party is that the announcement of our third store in town will be made during the party. The store will open late summer; we are taking over a store that recently closed."

"Great news and I like the party idea and it sounds like a fun theme."

"Glad you like it and please do not tell anyone about the new store; super secret and we have to keep it under wraps."

The next two weeks were typical days at the store; late spring always was a great shopping time here at Brissell's. For me, I was spending a bit less time at the store as Tiffany and I grew closer each day; I finally found a new love other than immersing myself into my job and career.

It was now Friday, one day prior to the party and Tiffany and I were eating at our favorite Italian restaurant. The dinner was over and our desserts were delivered and between bites I said, "Remember tomorrow is Brissell's party."

She replied, "I know dear, you told me about it back on the first and we spoke about it a couple more times over the last two weeks."

"I did? I don't recall talking about it."

You Must Be Kidding Me

"You did dear and I found this amazing year round Halloween shop and picked up our costumes earlier this week."

"What costumes did you pick?"

"Well my love, I will let it be a surprise."

"Okay, I am sure that whatever you picked will be awesome."

I was still thinking back to when were the other times I brought up the party and I really didn't remember telling her about them. Between bites of cheesecake with strawberries and drinking wine, Tiffany said, "You are thinking too hard, what's on your mind?"

Of course I wasn't going to tell her that I was forgetful, "I am thinking solely that I am the luckiest man."

"In what way?"

"I have you in my life."

Tiffany finished her cheesecake, smiled and then reached over with her fork and took a rather large bite of mine! This one bite she took was really a big deal, in the past I would have been rather upset with a date taking a bite of my cheesecake but now, I was fine with what Tiffany did, call it love. I continued

You Must Be Kidding Me

with my dessert and Tiffany smiled at me as she took yet another bite; I smiled back and we simply enjoyed the rest of the time at the restaurant.

We walked around the garden that surrounded the restaurant and held hands the whole time. I was so happy but still had lingering questions that I knew I wasn't going to get an answer to. We left and I drove her home and walked her to the front door, we kissed and I asked if I could come in but she said that she had to get up early the next day for work.

The next day was all about work at Brissell's and felt like I was dragging the whole day; I was looking forward to four and leaving for home and changing for the party. In addition to that, I had Tiffany on my mind and just five minutes before I received a call from Emery Knot.

"Hi Rob; hope you have a few minutes to talk."

I really didn't have the time, nor did I really want to talk to him. "Why not Emery, it isn't like I have anywhere to go."

"You are being sarcastic with me, aren't you Rob?"

"Yes, just getting ready to leave and get ready for the party."

You Must Be Kidding Me

"Well I have news for you; I received new information from Detective Lockhart."

"Really, it has been a while since we had the meeting with her and no news at all."

"I know, but she called earlier today and told me that she was being asked to move on from the cases of the missing employees. She said that there was absolutely nothing that had come up from the families or from within the store. In essence she said it was a dead case."

"Really Emery, it is a dead case?"

"Yes, that is what she said."

"Well, I hope that something turns up, I always have this in the back of my mind."

"Me too, by the way, what are you dressing up for the party?"

"Really don't know, Tiffany has this all planned out; I won't know till we get ready."

"Things seem to be moving pretty fast for you two, any plans like marriage?"

"Seriously not Knot, it took a while just for me to tell her that I'm in love with her. Marriage will happen but it is a ways off."

You Must Be Kidding Me

"Sure, that is what all men say but the women; well they have their own agenda and timeline."

"So those are your words of wisdom for me to be dealing with her?"

"Sure enough, we think we may be in control but forget it; Tiffany has you under her spell."

"Maybe so, but what a wonderful spell I am under and love her more than anything in the world."

"Alright Rob, it is after four and time to leave, see you later this evening."

"See you Emery and look forward to seeing you dressed up as?"

"If you think I am going to tell you, you are mistaken; it will be a surprise."

I hung up the phone and gathered some items off of my desk and then left for the parking structure and as I drove home, I wondered what on earth my dear Tiffany had planned for my costume. I knew one thing for sure; the costumes for both of us would be classy, totally unforgettable. Tiffany is so charming, how could our costumes be anything other than that? My thoughts were bouncing around in my head; this night was going to be a night for the record books. I was only a mile from the house when I received a call from Tiffany.

You Must Be Kidding Me

With a frantic voice, "Rob, Rob, where are you?"

"I am almost home, what's wrong?"

"I need you to turn around and go to my house, I just picked up the costumes and we need to change at my place; no time for me to go to yours."

"Calm down dear, it is no big deal and it is fine if we are late to the party."

She actually screamed back at me, "No Rob, we must be on time; we must be there by prior to six!"

I was so surprised by Tiffany's tone, "Relax, I am turning around right now and will be at your house in eight minutes."

"Make it six minutes Rob; I need you here and the sooner the better."

"Alright, I am on the way."

Tiffany hung up on me and I was not sure why she was so demanding that I hurry to get to her place. We had everything worked out this morning to meet at my house and no idea what happened to change our plans. This didn't make sense but I did what she requested and sped up and was at her house in five; nothing but green lights led me straight to her.

You Must Be Kidding Me

Tiffany was waiting outside her house; right next to the garage and in her hands was a large garment bag. I pulled into the driveway and she was reaching for the door even before the car was totally stopped.

I slammed on the breaks and screamed out to her as she was taking her seat in the car, "What is wrong with you?"

In a calm voice, "I am alright now, I am here with you and we will be able to change at the hotel, right before we get to the ballroom."

"You worried me Tiffany, you really did."

"Sorry dear, I wanted to be sure we had plenty of time to change and I was just a bit panic stricken."

I chuckled, "Just a bit?"

"Yes, just a bit."

We hardly said anything the rest of the drive to the hotel and I pulled into the driveway to the main lobby and up to valet. Tiffany grabbed the garment bag and placed it over her right arm and once again she was in high gear; I didn't have anything to do with her crazy actions; I calmly gave my keys to the valet driver and he gave me a receipt.

"Hurry up Rob, come on, we have to get going!"

You Must Be Kidding Me

I had to catch up with her as she was walking rather fast and when I did, I reached out for her left hand and grabbed it and squeezed it a bit. "Tiffany, please relax and let's not go crazy, this is a company party for Brissell's and it is not a big deal in the whole scheme of life. It is not like we have to punch a timecard."

Tiffany looked at her watch and stopped dead in her tracks, "Fine, we are doing fine and on time, I will chill."

I wasn't really convinced by her words, "Good dear, let's have a great time tonight and nothing and I do mean nothing will bring us down."

She caught her breath and I took the garment bag from her and together we proceeded to the restrooms that were around the corner from the ballroom. We went into the family bathroom and I placed the bag on the door hook and unzipped it and there they were the most amazing costumes I had ever seen.

I pulled off the hanger the first one and looked at Tiffany, "Is this yours or mine."

"Well dear, that is mine."

I handed it to her and then took mine off of the other hanger. We then took the costumes and pulled them over our heads and we took turns turning around, as we needed them zipped up from the back.

You Must Be Kidding Me

The zipper was all the way down to the ground and stopped right at our necks.

"Don't forget the masks Rob; we can put them on when we are ready to leave the room."

"Which mask is mine dear?"

Tiffany laughed, "Silly boy, the one with the red curly hair and with the big cheeks."

I put it on and then she put on hers, long blonde hair and with a charming child like face. I almost laughed out loud but held it in, "You look dashing my dear."

It was now ten till six and I grabbed the empty bag and opened the door and we popped out ready to make our entrance into the ballroom. We went around the corner and walked in and instantly received a standing ovation along with laughter. Now when I say laughter, I mean laughter like coming all the way up from your gut and out your mouth and this went on for a couple of minutes. I placed the garment bag down and was pleased that no one knew who was in these crazy costumes; we were previously directed by Ashley Kood to be totally covered up and not to say or do anything that would expose our true identity. I didn't even hold onto Tiffany as neither of us wanted to give anyone a clue as to who we were. I was hopeful that we would be able to take the masks off but that turned out not to be the case.

A man, not in costume took to the stage, "Good evening all, I am Henry Handifer, the Hotel Manager here at Stoneridge and I must say that looking around the room, you are all a sight to behold. Your store manager asked me to start the ball rolling by welcoming you and reminding you not to remove any part of your costumes as that would give away who you are and by no means, no talking, whooping it or anything else. Please mingle silently around the room for the next fifteen minutes and if you wish to be judged in the best costume contest, the signup sheet is located to the side of the bar. Sorry, the bar is closed till after the contest is over. If you sign up, all we need is the name of the character you are dressed up as. Regardless of signing up or not, please make your way to the chairs in front of the stage by six thirty."

Tiffany and I walked around the room; checking out all the costumes, some scary and others were, well just ordinary. We walked around the room for a few minutes and then I looked at her and nodded to my left and toward the bar. My lovely costumed Tiffany knew what I was indicating and we walked to the bar and signed up for the best costume contest. We then made our way to the area in front of the stage and took our seats in the second row; this was such an interesting site, all these other people dressed up in costumes and no one knew who was behind the masks. Maybe, I was sitting next to our store manager or the manager of our Cosmetics Department. The one and only person who I knew was of course my dear Tiffany and at this time, this was all that mattered.

More crazily dressed people took their seats and soon there were three rows of ten seats that were occupied. There were still others milling about the room but they seemed content doing their own thing and not wanting to be judged for the best costume. It was so odd, not a word was spoken and you could hear a pin drop. Then, everyone in the room both sitting at the stage and others throughout the room were surprised, a loud siren went off and Henry Handier took to the stage again and grabbed a portable microphone.

"Once again welcome one and all, we will start the costume contest in a few minutes but first, the instructions, please walk up to the stage from the right, one by one and when you reach the center, please do not talk, do not do any movements like flexing your muscles Superman or swinging your hips Miss Beauty Queen. You can slowly turn around twice but that is it; then exit the stage to your left and the next person can follow. Everyone who is seated, please look under your chairs and you will have a pencil and a scoring card, please use this to record the costumed character's name. Please score on a scale of one to ten for creativity and spookiness, and oh yes, you can whistle or clap if you can but no woo woo's or any other kind of talking. Now let's begin."

It started with Superman, then a bright red devil, and a construction worker, followed by a hideous looking something that I had no idea what he or she was supposed to be. A very pretty angel and then a person dressed up as a sailor and then a flight attendant. A werewolf, someone dressed up as a swimmer with a scary face and then not one but two vampires. Frankenstein took the stage and then a weird looking scientist who was obviously his creator. A clever costume of someone dressed as a tree and then a happy clown, a sad clown, a pretty witch, another witch with a long nose, a mummy and then a green alien. We were then treated to a tin man, a scarecrow, someone with what looked like regular work clothes but wielding a fake chainsaw and someone with one arm missing; too strange if you ask me.

Tiffany and I followed and there was laughter; I didn't know if this was a good thing or bad thing, I was the bottle of ketchup and Tiffany was the mustard. A fairy flitted by, another sweet looking witch, Batman was next and of course his sidekick Robin followed. Spiderman and then not one, not two but three strange costumes that were just, well weird and hard to describe. This was followed by a tall woman dressed like a movie star, a knight in full costume from head to toe, a guy dressed up as a girl wearing a blue and white dress with pink ruffles at the bottom and carrying a picnic basket, this was cute other than the guy had very hairy legs. A wolf of course followed the girl and finally it ended with someone dressed up as the Statue of Liberty.

After the Statue of Liberty left the stage, Henry Handifer was back, "Please finish your scoring and pass your scorecards to the right side of the rows and there will be someone who will collect them. Thank you all for being part of the contest; you will hear the results after dinner and during the dancing. Please enjoy the evening and now, those of you who have on masks may remove them, rather hard to eat dinner with them on. If you wish to remain anonymous, leave your masks on refrain from talking."

Tiffany and I had cutouts for our eyes and mouth so no one knew who we were and we remained quiet throughout dinner, which lasted till eight and the dancing lasted till ten. I had the time of my life dancing with the most beautiful bottle of mustard any bottle of ketchup could have. It was a fun evening and everyone seemed to be enjoying the festivities.

Henry Handier took to the stage and after tapping on the microphone to get everyone's attention he said, "Time for the results, we have a tie, will the angel and the picnic basket girl please come up to the stage."

You Must Be Kidding Me

There was applause and then, Henry said, "Please take off your mask or remove your makeup."

Hand towels were handed out by the hotel's staff and were used to remove the facial makeup for those who were not wearing masks. Tiffany and I took off our masks while others throughout the room took off their entire costumes and changed from their characters to; well, I couldn't believe who they really were.

Then, then right there on stage were Lenah and Emery Knot, not the angel or the girl with the picnic basket anymore! The room went crazy and I was flabbergasted. They left the stage and walked around the room and were congratulated by everyone they encountered. Tiffany and I were on our way to greet them when a weird thing happened, the werewolf jumped in front of us and threw a bucket of red drink on us and then quickly ran off. Tiffany and I were drenched; in fact our clothing underneath was quite damp as well. I was not too happy and wanted to do something but then Lenah and Emery came over to us and without them there, I might have done something I would regret.

Lenah felt terrible, "I am so sorry what happened, I know there is a changing room behind the stage, and you can dry off there and change into something dry."

You Must Be Kidding Me

Emery and Lenah then walked us behind the stage and to the room. I was rather surprised by their offer, "Thank you both but one little problem, our clothes underneath the costumes are damp and Tiffany and I don't have any clothes to change into."

Emery interjected, "No worry Rob, there is a change of clothing that you two can put on."

I replied to Emery, "There is what?"

Emery went on to say, "Rob, there were two costumes that were delivered here before the party started and the only instructions we were given was to hold onto them in case of a costume malfunction."

I looked at Tiffany and she hardly had a reaction. "Do you know anything about this dear?"

She shook her head no and Lenah went on to say, "Emery and I will leave the room and you can change; we will see you in a few minutes."

So my dearest Tiffany and I pulled off the ketchup and mustard costumes and our clothes underneath. We opened two bags, one marked 'for him' and the other marked 'for her'; the costumes were that of a prince and princess. We changed and walked out and at this time, only about fifteen people were still in the room and still in full costume. Those that were left yelled out their approval of what we were now wearing and I looked

You Must Be Kidding Me

at Tiffany and she looked back at me and we kissed, and kissed and hugged each other. The lights in the room dimmed and the dance floor was now lit up by two bright lights pointed at a turning crystal ball above it.

Very pleasant music started; Emery and Lenah were back on the stage and Emery said, "Will the prince and his princess please move to the center of the dance floor."

Tiffany and I walked hand in hand to the center, I then put my arms around her and she placed hers around me and we began to dance. This dance was long and when the music stopped, we continued to dance and then I said, "Tiffany, will you marry me?"

She hardly hesitated, "Yes Rob, I love you and yes, yes I will marry you."

The crowd heard it all and then everyone left in the room came up to the dance floor and hugged us, and offered their congratulations. Then, the witch took to the podium of the stage and took the mask off and everyone was so surprised, it was our Store Manager Ashley.

"First of all, I am so happy to be here with you tonight and congratulations Rob and Tiffany; you are indeed the most beautiful royal couple I have seen. I would like to make an announcement. Rob, please come up to the stage along with your bride."

You Must Be Kidding Me

I had no idea why Ashley wanted us on the stage; I took Tiffany's hand and went up to the stage and we stood next to Ashley.

"I have good news for you Rob; as you know, Brissell's took over a department store that recently closed. It will probably take a good three to four months to get it up and running and you are the manager that will bring the store to life. It is your store!"

I was speechless and that was rare for me. "Thank you so much Ashley and I, I am at a loss for words. One thing for sure, I look forward to the challenge."

"Emery took the microphone, "And Rob, there is more, will everyone take the stage and line up on each side of me."

It took a couple of minutes and Emery continued, "First and foremost, I want to introduce the angel, Detective Lenah Lockheart, she will continue."

"Thank you Emery. Back in January and right after your New Year's Eve party, I was given the case by our police department to investigate a missing person by the name of Crystal Champion and now…"

While Lenah was talking, the person dressed as a mummy began to take off the layers of cloth that covered her face and I was stunned to see who it was."

Lenah continued, "Let's welcome Crystal, Crystal Champion."

Emery went on to say, "Crystal actually moved out of town on New Year's Day to join an offshoot store of Brissell's and is the store's Sales Manager; she had to leave right away as she was set to start on the second. From what I have heard, they love her. Crystal is so happy she has this position; it was what she wished for."

I was stunned and smiled from ear to ear.

"Lenah smiled, "There is more Rob; twins it's your turn."

I was shocked, the masks of the two vampires were removed and it was the Kan sisters, Mary and Carol.

Emery was downright happy, "The Kan's were working with us for a couple of weeks when out of the blue they received a call from a job hunter who recruited them for a new hotel opening in Grand Junction Colorado. They had to fly out on the redeye flight right after the Valentine's Day party. Great job for them, they are co-managers of Guest Services and we wish them well."

You Must Be Kidding Me

"Still more Rob," Emery continued. Remember the team of three ladies that were going to plan the April Fools' Day party?

"Of course I do."

"Witch, please take off your mask."

There was a pause as there were two witches on stage, the pretty one and the other one with the long nose and they were standing next to each other and neither removed their masks.

Emery asked again, "Witch, please take off your mask, we need you to…!"

Lenah laughed and then said, "Emery, you need to be specific, which witch do you want to go first?"

"Oh, good point. How about at the count of three both witches take off your masks. Ready, one, two and…"

Lenah stopped the count, and if I recall, you had an interesting story that you told me about each. You told me that you and…"

Emery didn't let Lenah continue and yelled out "Three!"
Only one of the witches removed their mask and Emery introduced her, "Let's welcome Jinny Shapley."

You Must Be Kidding Me

Lenah interrupted, "No Knot not Shapley, it is Shapely, Jinny Shapely."

"I stand corrected. Other witch, please remove your mask."

I was totally surprised; it was Susan Shapley. Emery went on to say, "Susan married and left the company to be with her new husband, Barney Nu. They still live here, and Barney is working for a marketing company; they were on their honeymoon but came back a day early just to be here. And let's give it up to the other witch who is Jinny Shapely and she left Brissell's for a new job out of town; we tracked her down and she came back just for this night. Not sure what she is doing but it was kind that she found the time to be here tonight."

Lenah grabbed the microphone, "How about if we move on to the tin man. Tin Man please remove your mask so we can see who you are."

I was waiting to see who this was and it took a bit for the elaborate mask to come off. Then to my delight, it was Wendy Wood.

Lenah was laughing, "Remember Rob that you worked with Wendy Wood in Kansas. Well, she is back at the same hotel but now it is part of a chain and she is their Regional Manager. They have ten hotels in the chain. Back to you Emery."

You Must Be Kidding Me

"More surprises Rob; Lenah and I fell in love at first sight when we had our meeting regarding Crystal's disappearance. We wound up flying out to Las Vegas right before the Valentine's Day party; Lenah is dressed appropriately tonight, she is truly an angel, I love her so much."

"I love you too Emery and now Rob, Ashley has more to add. Ashley, please take over."

Ashley let out a sigh and a few tears ran down from her right eye, she then went on to say, "Lenah is my younger sister and she had been living out of town but moved back here last year and was living with me and my husband till she married Emery. I love you little sis."

Lenah couldn't hold back the tears, "Love you too big sis."

Ashley had tears in her eyes as well, "Remember Rob when you met Tiffany, well that was a bit of a planned thing,"

I was so shocked with all that was going on and this came out of nowhere, "How could that be planned? She was slipping and bumped into me and I fell down. How could that be planned?"
"Simple Rob, I didn't know that Tiffany was going to be at the New Year's Eve party, she was there with her best friend, Susan Sed So."

You Must Be Kidding Me

"Alright, but you couldn't stage that whole thing?"

"It was just a coincidence that she was there but when I saw her with Susan, I came up with the idea to have that guy purposely bump into you."

"That clumsy guy right?"

"You are catching on and there is more. You see Rob, Tiffany is my cousin and I felt for such a long time that you and her would be perfect together."

"Okay but I still don't get it."

"I told the guy that I would pay him fifty dollars if he would stage the bumping into Tiffany causing her to bump into you. I had no idea that the little bump I was looking for would wind up the way that it did however, that turned out to be the best fifty dollars spent on anything."

This whole night was something else and there were still others on the stage that had yet to reveal themselves. One thing for sure, the missing employees were accounted for, "So Ashley, who else is on stage with us?"

"Emery, introduce the others please."

"Thank you; let's just have them take off their masks or costumes one by one."

You Must Be Kidding Me

"Great idea, everyone, please show us who you are."

One by one, we saw who was who. The flight attendant was Susan Sed So and Pam Whaz was the scarecrow. Superman was Bonnie Whyt and Shandra Lance was the creature that I had no idea what she was. The werewolf was last to take off the mask; it was our regional VP over sales, Theresa Day. All of this was so remarkable and I walked over to each and everyone on the stage and gave them hardy hugs.

After the last hug, I took the hand of my beautiful princess, my future wife and we went to the center of the stage; I didn't take the microphone, my voice would carry without it. "I am so shocked, astonished, full of happiness and so many other emotions about this whole evening and have no idea where to begin but one question that I have and it is probably the most important, how did this all come to be?"

Ashley came over to me and hugged me and reached for the microphone. "This evening was going to be a spring into summer party but we changed the theme when the job for you was finalized; a few of us got together and came up with the Halloween theme. Originally we were going to have a normal party and announce your new job but that all changed. We decided to pull off this practical joke on you and the whole thing started at the New

You Must Be Kidding Me

Year's Eve party. There were so many moving parts to pull this off and I doubt I'll remember them all but the first one came about when Crystal told me about her new job and having to leave right away, this is what got the whole joke started.

I talked to others during that party and from there the idea grew and over the months, we just kept adding to it as the others had changes in their lives that resulted in them leaving Brissell's. It just all worked out like magic. By the way Rob, Lenah was recruited by your Admin Assistant, Sheila Koffee from a party company. Lenah has acting experience doing summer theatre and she was the key to the whole practical joke. She pulled this off first thing on the Monday after the New Year's Eve party, which was on Friday and prior to her going to your house. Go figure, Lenah and Emery fell in love."

I was somewhat speechless, "So Ashley, everyone pulled off this elaborate prank on me?"

"We sure did Rob."

I kissed my bride to be; "You planned the whole thing with the werewolf didn't you?"

Tiffany smiled, "I had no idea what was going on, totally shocked as you were."

I leaned over to her and after yet another kiss and with a somewhat shaky voice, "To all of you who totally surprised me, I am so happy to be with my Brissell's family and the woman of my dreams. I don't know what else to say other than, you must be kidding me!"

A waiter and waitress walked up to the stage and had champagne for us, Ashley commented, "We sure pulled this practical joke off and from all of us, congratulations on your new job and we will miss you. To you and Tiffany we offer our best wishes. Now, everyone bottoms up, good night and drive home safely."

Made in the USA
Monee, IL
15 August 2021